The Queen's English
(HIGH TAW TAWK PRAWPAH-LEAH)

THE QUEEN'S ENGLISH

(HIGH TAW TAWK PRAWPAH-LEAH)

with

SIR VERE BRAYNE d'HEMMIDGE
and
LADY MAYNA BRAYNE d'HEMMIDGE

by
Dorgan Rushton

PELHAM BOOKS
London

First published in Great Britain by
Pelham Books Ltd
44 Bedford Square
London WC1B 3DP
1985

Text © Dorgan Rushton 1985
Illustrations © William Rushton 1985

Design and typography by Tony Fahy

All Rights Reserved. No part of this publication may be reproduced, stored in a
retrieval system, or transmitted, in any form or by any means, electronic, mechanical,
photocopying, recording or otherwise, without the prior permission of the Copyright owners.

British Library Cataloguing in Publication Data

Rushton, Dorgan
The Queen's English : (high taw tawk prawpah-leah): with Sir Vere Brayne d'Hemmidge and Mayna Brayne d'Hemmidge
1. English language—Spoken English—Anecdotes, facetiae, satire, etc.
I. Title
428.3'0207   PE1095

ISBN 0 7207 1605 5

Typeset by MS Filmsetting Limited, Frome, Somerset
Printed and bound in Great Britain by Butler & Tanner Ltd, Frome and London

CONTENTS

Preface 9

Acknowledgments 11

How to Use This Book 12

THE THIRTEEN STEPS

Basic Training 17

Exercise 1 – Posture 19
Exercise 2 – Gargling 20
Exercise 3 – Grunting 22
Exercise 4 – Gritting the Teeth 22
Exercise 5 – Shouting 25
Exercise 6 – Hail and Farewell 26
Exercise 7 – First Phrases 28
Exercise 8 – Vowel Practice 28
Exercise 9 – A Poem 30
Exercise 10 – Numbers 31
Exercise 11 – The Alphabet 32
Exercise 12 – The Calendar 33
Exercise 13 – Parts of the Body 34

Field Trip No. 1: A Simple Outdoor Exercise to Inspire Confidence 36

PARTY PIECES

Home Improvements 39

About the House 40
Field Trip No. 2: At the Pub 54

Food 60
Field Trip No. 3: Doing Your Marketing 67

England 71
Field Trip No. 4: Sporting Fixtures 74

All About London 84
Field Trip No. 5: Round Town 87
Field Trip No. 6: Harrods 94

Style 96
Field Trip No. 7: Name Dropping 107
Field Trip No. 8: Place Dropping 113

The Passing Out Parade 120
Field Trip No. 9: The Garden Party 121

The Last Word from Lady Mayna 127

IT IS WITH THE GREATEST PLEASURE THAT I DEDICATE THIS BOOK, *THE QUEEN'S ENGLISH*, TO THE ROYAL FAMILY, WHO GIVE US SUCH FINE EXAMPLES OF HOW BEST TO SPEAK OUR WONDERFUL LANGUAGE.

   I NAME THIS BOOK *THE QUEEN'S ENGLISH (HIGH TAW TAWK PRAWPAH-LEAH)* AND I BLESS ALL THOSE WHO SAIL IN HER. MY HUSBAND AND I HAVE, FOR MANY YEARS, BEEN AT WAR . . .

EDITOR'S NOTE: Unfortunately, the rest of Lady Mayna's long dedication seems to have been lost in vintage champagne stains. I know you will regret this as much as I do.

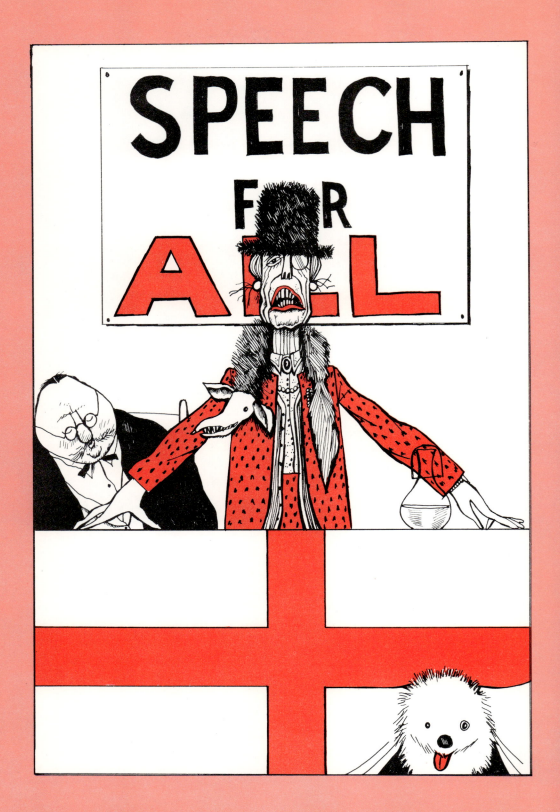

PREFACE

LADY MAYNA WRITES: What on earth has happened to this country of ours? Why is there no speech training? Why is there still a language barrier between the classes? There are millions of English people living here today who, from their speech, might as well be foreigners. One cannot understand a word they say. I write this book to rectify the situation. Of course, my husband, Sir Vere, maintains that he has no desire to find out what the people are saying, but I say that being forearmed is being forewarned. As President of S.F.A. (Speech For All) I felt it was my duty, and so set about this enormous task with a will.

This book should have been on the school curriculum one hundred years ago. An oversight, dare I say a deliberate mistake, that I have pointed out to the Government again and again. Why should not the lower classes learn to speak properly? After all, talk is cheap. To date, we at S.F.A. have written over five thousand letters to those responsible and received not one reply. The Prime Minister's often quoted remark about throttling me will not deter me. All my life people have been saying the same thing, to the same effect. If you never see this book, you will know why.

Chamberlain knew, and did nothing about it. I have it on good authority that the piece of paper he was waving above his head in 1939 was one of my letters. Churchill knew, and there was a short period of time during the forties when he looked very shaky indeed. Macmillan refused to acknowledge me at all. Wilson, Heath and Thatcher, despite their desperate need for this book, also chose to ignore the mounting correspondence. So, I have been forced to go public. The repercussions could be appalling. Many may go berserk.

The staff at Pelham, at first, were almost speechless at the magnitude of my project and understandably in awe of the proposed book. However, after simply hundreds of letters and several thousand phone calls, I finally gave them my advance payment and now the book is ready to grace the shelves of millions of hovels all over this once great country.

We're in a fever of excitement down at the Manor. My daughter, poor Sybil, says that we may even get on the *best cellar list*, which she says is crucial. Of course, we do have a very good cellar, certainly one of the best in the country, where Sir Vere spends many happy hours, from what one can hear, assiduously practising his vowel sounds.

I look forward keenly to being at last able to talk to you all, when you have finished this course of speech lessons.

Chins up, keep a stiff upper lip and jolly good luck.

Lady Mayna Brayne-d'Hemmidge

ACKNOWLEDGMENTS

The S.F.A. wishes to acknowledge the sterling work of Professor A. Lauder in this field among the Aboriginals of Australia

How to use this book

LADY MAYNA WRITES: The staff at Pelham have suggested that I write a short piece for you on how to use this book.

I can heartily recommend the drawing room as a good place to practise, in the afternoon, when the voice is at its best, possibly before or after the parlour maid has brought in the tea tray. You should hold the book about eighteen inches from your face, and have it covered with a clear plastic sheet to protect it from the spitting that may occur during your basic training.

The book itself is clearly divided into two sections. Part one, The Thirteen Steps, consists of loosening-up exercises, jowl control and noise encouragement. When you have mastered these, you may move on to part two, Party Pieces. Party Pieces, as the name suggests, is a gay approach to learning to speak properly in everyday conversation, whether at home, in the restaurant, on the sports field, shopping, globe trotting or even at Buckingham Palace. All the words and phrases you are ever likely to need are to be found within, to take you from the nursery to the grave. Many of the chapters have recommended Field Trips, which will prove to you how your Modified Language is progressing. For those of you wishing to attempt an Honours Degree, a slightly harder course has been set. You will also find within this book a book-mark which, when used in the manner shown, will be an invaluable aid to pronunciation. Do use it.

I am divulging for the first time a list of places where I have shopped for many years, and though, unfortunately, it is against our Field Trip rules to mention my name, perhaps a flourish or two of the book may help you get someone's attention.

Some of you may find that you have to save your money for a month or so in order to afford a few of the Field Trips, but think on this for a moment: how much would it have cost you to go to Eton? Which all goes to prove that in this country at the moment, there is no such thing as free speech.

HOW NOT TO USE YOUR BOOK-MARK

The Thirteen Steps

Audrey Ffoote-ffoote whore hed hah bawk-mawk weird tah tith taw iamprawv hah vile signeds — end ian sikhs marnths geened ay laugh-lear egg-scent end lawst tin stain. *

BEFORE AFTER

* Audrey Ffoote-ffoote who had her book-mark wired to her teeth to improve her vowel-sounds — and in six months gained a lovely accent and lost ten stone.

BASIC TRAINING
BEE-SICK TREE-KNEEING

Should you be from:

America
Australia
Canada
New Zealand
South Africa
South of the Thames
North of Watford
East of Anthony Eden

the S.F.A. recommends the following obligatory speech training exercises to you.

S.F.A. Warning: Do not, under any circumstances, attempt any of the phrases in this book until you have mastered these basic steps. To do so could seriously damage your health.

We wish to make it known that we cannot absolutely guarantee perfect results for foreigners from member countries of the E.E.C. because of their peculiar vowels.

Exercise 1

POSTURE

PAWS-TIOR

1 Stand in the centre of the room
2 Look at the ceiling
3 Put your hands behind your back
4 Rock slowly backwards and forwards on your heels
5 Clench your teeth

When you are in no danger of falling over
6 Walk stiff-legged to fireplace
7 Resume exercise

When you can do this for hours on end you are ready to combine it with Exercise 2.

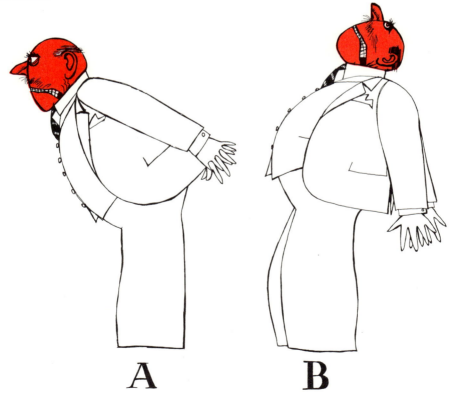

A   **B**

EXERCISE 2

GARGLING
GAWGLING

Do not use water for this exercise.
British phlegm is recommended.

What we are looking for here is a good strong sound that can be used as a preface to any sentence, which alerts those present that words will shortly be uttered, or, in mid-sentence, that there is more to come.

1   Throw back the head and gargle some long '**Ahs**' in any musical key of your choice for at least *one minute*.

2   Run up and down the musical scale for *two minutes* (taking breaths where necessary). As you practice, you will see that you can register grave doubt, agreement, enthusiasm and even sympathy in this manner.

3   Practise for *three minutes* in the Upper Register. Think of the sound of a diving bomber. This is particularly useful for moments of recollection or recognition. *Viz:* ten seconds of diving bomber plus the name of object or person remembered or recognised:

a) **knneeeeeeaaAAAAAAGH! +HENCORK!**
b) **KNNNEEEEeeeaaaaaagh! +ETON 1958!**

Practise those crescendos.

EXERCISE 3

GRUNTING

GRAHNTING

A grunt is an invaluable addenda to your vocabulary. It serves as a greeting to staff, etc., particularly when married to The Gargle.

The sound of The Grunt can be best described as that of a pig clearing its throat, as I discovered one day down by the piggery when I held a long and interesting conversation with what I thought was Sir Vere, until I remembered he'd gone to Wincanton Races.

EXERCISE 4

GRITTING THE TEETH

GREETING THAH TIERTH

Gritting the teeth is similar to teeth clenching in Exercise 1. However, you may find you have trouble speaking whilst clenching.

Try this simple exercise

1 Put the patented bookmark *cum* jowl exerciser attached to this book between your teeth as illustrated. Clench firmly and read the racing results from Pontefract.

You should soon hear some marked improvement.

At this juncture it is interesting to point out that one of the greatest exponents of the Modified Language is our own Prince Charles, who, as a result of more than thirty years of correct speaking, has extremely well-developed jowl muscles.

EXERCISE 5

SHOUTING

SHITEING

We admit that this can be most difficult for the beginner. But shouting with teeth firmly clenched can be achieved with practice.

Grit teeth and without moving them shout **'Waiter, waiter!'** over and over again until your jowls ache. If you are in the correct position, it should sound like **'Wheateh, wheateh!'** (as in Weetabix without the bix).

EXERCISE 6

HAIL AND FAREWELL
HEEL END FEAR-WILL

With teeth clenched, say loudly and clearly:

1. Hell-eah
2. Heh-leo
3. Heh-leooooooooooooh
4. Heh-leooooooooooooh thah

5. High ah yaw?
6. High yaw?

7. Aim faine

8. Gawd mawning
9. Gawd deh
10. Gawd nate
11. Gawd bay

Your first words!
Say the above into a tape recorder. Listen for the exciting results.

EXERCISE 7

FIRST PHRASES

FAST FREEZERS

Remember to keep those teeth clenched.

Water lahv-leah deh	What a lovely day
Water maled nate	What a mild night
Weir Sue gled yorkered calm	We're so glad you could come
Water naice hice	What a nice house
Wart chaw-ming grinds	What charming grounds
High naice yaw lawk	How nice you look
War Dior lake taw daunts?	Would you like to dance?

Learn these phrases by heart; they will prove invaluable to you. Combine with Exercise 6 – the results will astound you!

EXERCISE 8

VOWEL PRACTICE

VILE PRIK-TEASE

Say the following loudly and clearly into your tape recorder:

1 High nigh brine kye

2 Nigh ease theh tame faw awl gawd min taw calm taw theh eed orv theh paw-teah

3 **Ay steech Ian tame seives nane**

4 **Min seal-dawm meek paw-sis et ghels haw weir glaw-sis (Dawthy Porker)**

5 **Hee haw hairsy-teats ease lawst**

Now play back to find out what you are saying.
If you have no tape recorder, have a friend or a servant listen to you.
Members of the family may care to join in the game.

(*Translations are given below.*)

Translation of Exercise 8

1 How now brown cow
2 Now is the time for all good men to come to the aid of the party
3 A stitch in time saves nine
4 Men seldom make passes at girls who wear glasses (Dorothy Parker)
5 He who hesitates is lost

EXERCISE 9

A POEM

AY PAY-EM

Another excellent exercise to do with your tape recorder:

Ay wahn-deared lane-leah es ay Clyde,	I wandered lonely as a cloud,
Thet flirt-sawn hay, aw veals end heels,	That floats on high, o'er vales and hills,
Win awl et wahnse ay sewer cried,	When all at once I saw a crowd,
Ay haste awv gale-dean daffydeals	A host of golden daffodils
WADSWATH	WORDSWORTH

EXERCISE 10

NUMBERS

NAHM-BAHS

Wahn	One
Taw	Two
Threh	Three
Faw	Four
Fave	Five
Sikhs	Six
Sivven	Seven
Eat	Eight
Nane	Nine
Tin	Ten
Ill-ivvin	Eleven
Tweirlv	Twelve
Thah-tea-urn	Thirteen
Twin-tier	Twenty
Hahn-drid	Hundred
Thighs-end	Thousand
Meal-yawn	Million

EXERCISE 11

THE ALPHABET

THEH ELF-ORBIT

Air-Beer-Seer-Dear	A-B-C-D
Ear-If-Jeer-Each	E-F-G-H
Ay-Gee-Care-Ill	I-J-K-L
Im-In-Ae-Pay	M-N-O-P
Kew-Aw-Is-Tear	Q-R-S-T
Yaw-Veer-Dah-bull Yaw	U-V-W
Icks-Way-Zid	X-Y-Z

EXERCISE 12

THE CALENDAR
THAH CAR LINDA

Marnth-sawv thah yah	Months of the year
Jin-yaw-airy	January
Fib-raw-airy	February
Mawch	March
E-prill	April
Me	May
Jawn	June
Jaw-lay	July
Awgst	August
Sip-timbah	September
Auk-tow-bah	October
Neo-vim-bah	November
D-sim-bah	December

Dees awv thah weirk	Days of the week
Marne-dear	Monday
To-yaws-dear	Tuesday
Wins-dear	Wednesday
Thahs-dear	Thursday
Fray-dear	Friday
Setter-dear	Saturday
Sarne-dear	Sunday

EXERCISE 13

PARTS OF THE BODY

PAWTS AWV THEH BAWDY

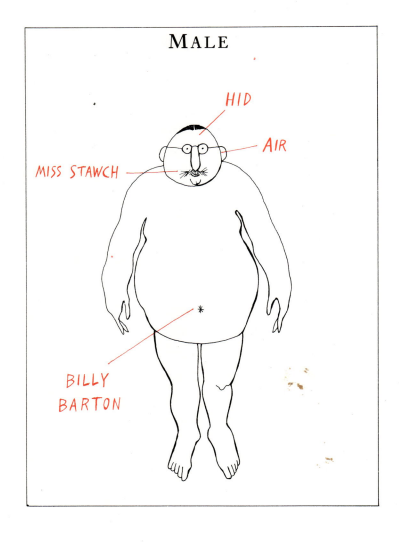

LADY MAYNA WRITES: We live in permissive times and, having always been considered a 'Modern Woman', I have fearlessly agreed to allow nudity in this book. I realize that this has caused muttering amongst some of my so-called friends, and if I know them, it will continue to so do. However, I am not, as they imply, climbing on the band-wagon of literary licentiousness. The drawings have artistic merit and are necessary for this dictionary. They are to be looked on as merely a basic lesson in anatomy. So pigs to you, Mrs Cooper.

It is true that Sir Vere and I were used as the models for these sketches, but we wish it known that we were not unclothed at the time.

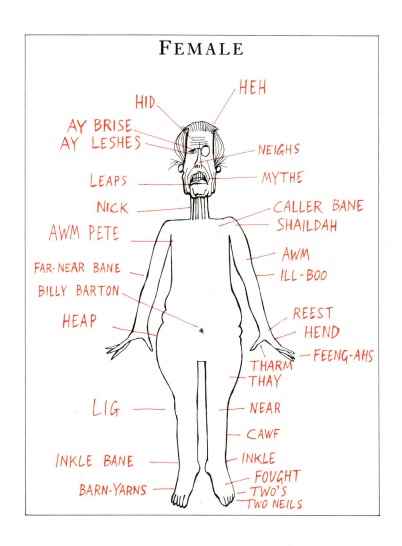

FIELD TRIP No. 1

A SIMPLE OUTDOOR EXERCISE
TO INSPIRE CONFIDENCE

1 Stand to attention on any London street corner
2 Look at the clouds
3 Gargle
4 Hold umbrella arm aloft
5 Shout:

TEX-YAH!

Party Pieces

Home Improvements
(WHOM EEMPROOV-MINCE)

By now you should be ready for some really practical work.

Most people prefer to do their practice in the privacy of their own home. This is, indeed, a wise precaution as we have had the odd report of falling over and one unfortunate case of lock jaw. Because of this, we begin our lessons with sentences suitable for use indoors. However, we do earnestly commend that you *get out into the garden at the first possible moment.*

To this end, we have included a gardening section as a supplement to your Home Work.

Do not become a closet speaker!

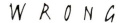

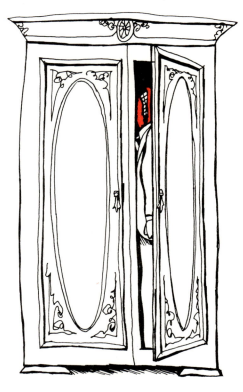

About the House
AY-BITE THEH HICE

LADY MAYNA WRITES: Perfect speech begins in the bosom of one's family, like Charity and good manners. I entreat you to practice your Modified Language at every opportunity about the house. You may begin as quietly as you wish, but as you hear the results, as you see the looks of amazement on family, servants' and friends' faces, your joy and your noise level will know no bounds. Soon, shouting will become the norm for you.

I have listed correct pronunciations for many things around the home, as well as phrases you may use for the servants, for social events and for intimate family occasions, so that you may be covered for every possible eventuality.

STAFF
STAWF

Bart-lah	Butler
Shoe-fah	Chauffeur
Fought-men	Footman
Grawm	Groom
Paw-law mead	Parlour maid
Dearly	Daily
Cork	Cook
Hice kipper	Housekeeper

HOUSEHOLD NAMES
HICE-HAILED NEEMS

In-trahn-saul	Entrance hall
Het wreck	Hat rack
Willing-torn boughts	Wellington boots

Tilly-foon	Telephone
V.C. Taws bawk	Visitors' book

Maw-kneeing rrm   **Morning room**

Caw-pit	Carpet
Sit-here	Settee
Horney mince	Ornaments
Floor-ill Dick-aw-Asians	Floral decorations
Kees-mint weirn-doos	Casement windows

Leaving rrm   **Living room**

Porky	Parquet
Rahg	Rug
Sue-fah	Sofa
Ian-teak fah-neat-yaw	Antique furniture
Fearm-leah ear-lumes	Family heirlooms
Pee-ah-noh	Piano

Day-kneeing rrm   **Dining room**

Ben-quitting teable	Banquetting table
Tear-piss-treah	Tapestry
Cheers	Chairs
Jaw-gin seal-vah	Georgian silver

Beal-yawd rrm   **Billiard room**

Hice pentahs	House painters
Dahst shits	Dust sheets

Ache pen-held lay-brair-ear   **Oak-panelled library**

Rating disk	Writing desk
Dis-petch kees	Despatch case
Bawk shilves	Book shelves

Cawn-sah-vah-treah   **Conservatory**

Fine-tin	Fountain
Stet-yaws	Statues
Fringe daws	French doors
Jaw-dear-near	Jardinière

Tray-fear-rrm   Trophy room

Eel-offence tasks	Elephant's tusks
Staffed hid	Stuffed head
Tay-gah skean	Tiger skin

Men stah-kiss   Main staircase

Eggs-mince-stah	Axminster
Lending	Landing
Benny-stores	Bannisters

Maw-stah bid rrm   Master bedroom

Faw paster	Four poster
Ada-dine	Eiderdown
Trizer-prayers	Trouser press
Far-please	Fireplace
Chembah port	Chamber pot

Bawth rrm   Bathroom

Leveh-treah	Lavatory
Shire	Shower
Bee-sin	Basin
Kendal	Candle
Tiles	Towels
Tailored peeper	Toilet paper

Nahs-reah wheeng   Nursery wing

Caught	Cot
Rawking whores	Rocking horse
Nen-iah	Nanny
Dawls hice	Dolls' house
Mawdle real-weir	Model railway
Deenkie tays	Dinky toys

Sah-vince kwortahs   Servants' quarters
Key-chin   Kitchen

Pain drissah	Pine dresser
Sores-pins	Saucepans
Corker	Cooker

USEFUL PHRASES (SERVANTS)
YAWS-FALL FREEZERS (SAH-VINCE)

Wad yaw shoe ah gists Ian-taw thah _____ ?	Would you show our guests in to the _____ ?
Teak thah bee-ships het bawx taw thah _____	Take the Bishop's hat box to the _____
Hes inny-worn Vic-humed thah _____ yit?	Has anyone vacuumed the _____ yet?
Queek! Ay peer-cork ease rahning ay-mawk Ian thah _____	Quick! A peacock is running amok in the _____
Thah carnels Ian thah _____	The Colonel's in the _____
Wahn awv thah dawgs hes darn sahm-theeng awn thah _____	One of the dogs has done something on the _____
Yaw me sahv teah Ian thah _____	You may serve tea in the _____
Wheel hev sah-pah Ian thah _____	We'll have supper in the _____
Weir sim tev mace Ian thah _____	We seem to have mice in the _____
Thah _____ nids dah-sting	The _____ needs dusting
Wart ease thet did fear-it daw-ing Ian thah _____ ?	What is that dead ferret doing in the _____ ?
Whore ease rear-spawn-Sybil faw paw-leashing thah _____ ?	Who is responsible for polishing the _____ ?

FAMILY CONVERSATION PIECES
FEAR-MEALY CAWN-VAH-SAY-SHONE PIERCES

Brick-fist	**Breakfast**
Water weeta daw taw-deh?	What are we to do today?
Aim awf taw gofe	I'm off to golf
Aim gaying taw may clarb	I'm going to my club

43

Jest pawping rind taw thah parb	Just popping round to the pub
Aim gaying tevver lawket theh hawsers	I'm going to have a look at the horses
Weege caw wheel yaw beer teaking?	Which car will you be taking?
Ay heat screm-build igs	I hate scrambled eggs
Warts hair-pinned tall thah kitsch-sherry?	What's happened to all the kedgeree?
Stawfs deh awf	Staff's day off

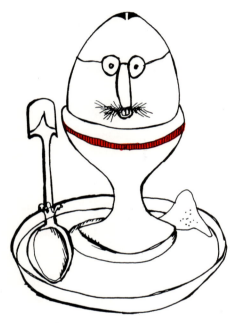

Aid lake ay wahd weeth yaw	I'd like a word with you
Wez thet theh daw-bill?	Was that the door-bell?
Aim tebblah wud ay-bite _____	I'm terribly worried about _____
Aw weir drissing faw dean-gnaw?	Are we dressing for dinner?
Weirds fell may	Words fail me
Fay wuz yaw, aid war-cheat	If I was you, I'd watch it
Weirs yaw faw-thah gawn?	Where's your father gone?

Sah-pah — **Supper**

Inny-theeng awn thah bawx taw-nate?	Anything on the box tonight?
Aim Brian-dawf	I'm browned off

Sue May	So am I
Ahnkle hairy ease calming taw teah	Uncle Harry is coming to tea
Hes inny-worn sin may neating?	Has anyone seen my knitting?
Ay fill ay ken sea-flear-sea...	I feel I can safely say...
Cork ease hevving N.F.Ear weeth thah grey-sir	Cook is having an affair with the grocer
Ay thiernk shis awn hit	I think she's on heat
Warts these mit?	What's this meat?
Ill-boo-sawf theh teable	Elbows off the table
Awnt floor-rinse ease teaking Ian peeing-gists	Aunt Florence is taking in paying guests
Whore warnts ear geem awv ————	Who wants a game of ————
Weirs yaw faw-thah dee-sah-paired taw?	Where's your father disappeared to?
Ale of yaw	I love you

FAMILY NAMES
FEAR-MEALY NEEMS

May waif	My wife
May jailed	My child
May has-binned	My husband
May sea-star	My sister
May bra-thah	My brother
Sport	Spot
Raver	Rover
Dulling	Darling
May pit	My pet
Mahm-meah	Mummy
Deadie	Daddy

SOCIAL CHIT-CHAT (Guests)
SUE-SHELL CHEAT-CHET (Gists)

May cord	My card
Weir aw yaw leaving nigh?	Where are you living now?
Dior plea breach?	Do you play bridge?
Warten ear-gnaw-mice gofe-beg yaw hev	What an enormous golf bag you have
Thah wheeng caw-mahn-dahs nior lig hes bin ay greet sark-sis	The Wing Commander's new leg has been a great success
May gawd! Wart hes sheer dahn taw hah heh?	My God! What has she done to her hair?
Theh veekah ease ay chaw-ming parson	The vicar is a charming person
Ave hard here hed ay nah-vus Brie-ache-dine	I've heard he had a nervous breakdown
Dior haunt?	Do you hunt?
His gawn twerk fawrah farm Ian that C.T.	He's gone to work for a farm in the city
These hice hes bin Ian thah fear-mealy faw thah pawst faiv hahn-drid yahs	This house has been in the family for the past five hundred years
Weir hale-ding ay charm-bull seal father judge	We're holding a jumble sale for the Church
His bin awf he's rawkah faw yahs, may D.R. fillow	He's been off his rocker for years, my dear fellow
Weir nid maw min lake thet Ian thah gavah-mint	We need more men like that in the Government
Aim edicted taw dinner-steer	I'm addicted to Dynasty
Dior worch eight awl?	Do you watch at all?
Ay N. J. Dilys	I enjoy Dallas
Theh mare-jar hed ay virry gawd wahr	The Major had a very good war

Lawks lake weire Ian fawrah stawm, dane-tu-theenk?

Looks like we're in for a storm, don't you think?

Theh cheery blaw-sem ease ite ah-leah these yah

The cherry blossom is out early this year

GARDENING SUPPLEMENT
GORDONING SAH-PLAH-MINT

Ian yaw gordon	In your garden
Theh rules	The Rolls
Theh deemlah	The Daimler
Thawstn	The Austin
Droar-breach	Drawbridge
Mate	Moat
Sworn	Swan
Swee-ming Paul	Swimming pool
Steer-bull	Stable
Tens caught	Tennis court
Nane hale gofe cause	Nine-hole golf course
Peer-corks	Peacocks
Awna-mintel pawned	Ornamental pond
Ruse-sah-bah	Rose arbor
Rook-ah-rare	Rockery
Caw-near-shone	Carnation
Paw-plahs	Poplars
Rare-bits	Rabbits
Beers	Bees
Sneels	Snails
Poor-peas	Poppies
Frawgs	Frogs

Bards	Buds
Baind-weird	Bindweed
Dearsy	Daisy
Milly barg	Mealy bug
Ian sicked	Insect
Fart-ill-eye-sore	Fertilizer
Seeker-tours	Secateurs
Gordon pissed	Garden pest
In theh grin hice	**In the greenhouse**
Sueing	Sowing
Pawting	Potting
Plenting	Planting
Hawdning awf	Hardening off
Grin flay	Green fly
Wall-ear air-feed	Woolly aphid
Lee-faw-pah	leaf hopper
Slahg	Slug
Spree	Spray
Ian sicked asade	Insecticide
Meal-Dior	Mildew
Bleck mailed	Black mould

USEFUL PHRASES (STAFF)
YAWS-FALL FREEZERS (STAWF)

Nigh ease theh tame taw sue thah ＿＿＿

Now is the time to sow the ＿＿＿

Till theh gordnah thars air ship Ian thah ____	Tell the gardener there's a sheep in the ____
Theh ____ aw bed these yah	The ____ are bad this year
Frawst gawt may ____	Frost got my ____
Theh ____ nid ay spree	The ____ need a spray
Theh males hev darg hales Ian theh ____	The moles have dug holes in the ____
Yawken tahn theh haze awf nigh, may gawd men	You can turn the hose off now, my good man
Theh gate hes ear-ten may ____	The goat has eaten my ____
Thahs messes awv maws awl Ava theh ____	There's masses of moss all over the ____
Theh Avis gawn med	The ivy's gone mad
These ____ cord door weeth-ah prawn	This ____ could do with a prune
Theh ____ gawt Ian taw thah fraught tray	The ____ got into the fruit tree
Ease these ay weird?	Is this a weed?
Whores ket ease thet?	Who's cat is that?
Bleck sport ease teaking Ava theh ____	Black spot is taking over the ____

 ## GENERAL CHAT (NOT STAFF)

GIN-RAWL CHET (NOUGHT STAWF)

Lawks lake wren	Looks like rain
Wren ease virry gawd faw theh crawps	Rain is very good for the crops
Theh lay-licks Ian blawm	The lilac's in bloom
Keeper-bee-litty brine leed ite ah grinds	Capability Brown laid out our grounds
Gawd lawd! Theh lend raver hairs rahn Ava ah Gordon names!	Good Lord! The Land Rover has run over our garden gnomes!

Aim ay mortar taw mitches	I'm a martyr to midges
Ay theenk psalm any-mell hairs dade Ian theh sah-mah hice	I think some animal has died in the summer house
Whars theh humpah? Weir gaying tev ay peak-neek bay theh leak	Where's the hamper? We're going to have a picnic by the lake
Ay Raleigh door hev air grin tharm	I really do have a green thumb
Theh hair-bare-shus baw-dah lawks laugh-lear	The herbaceous border looks lovely
Theh sworns aw beer-heaving lake Kenny Balls	The swans are behaving like cannibals
Ay ket hes ear-ten theh portreach Ian thah pah-tray	A cat has eaten the partridge in the pear tree
May hay-drean-jaws awnt wart their yaws taw beer	My hydrangeas aren't what they used to be
Shawking withah weir hevving	Shocking weather we're having
Paw Sybil hes bin rahn dine bay theh hivvy railer	Poor Sybil has been run down by the heavy roller
High laugh-lear theh snay lawks awn theh gordnah	How lovely the snow looks on the gardener

FIELD TRIP NO. 2
AT THE PUB
IT THEH PARB

By now you should be really keen to take your Modified Language into the field proper. It is one thing to have tried it at home or in front of the gardener, it is quite another to let fly in a public place. This is why we recommend a visit to a hostelry. Take this book with you, in a plain brown paper wrapper, and armed with the phrases on the following pages, you may find yourself the focal point of a good deal of admiration and envy. Take with you about £100.

LADY MAYNA WRITES: I have used London as a centre of operations for all our field trips as it is frightfully easy to get to with the new motorways, and even if you haven't a chauffeur, I believe there's something called Play Away Day cheap returns which I was told to mention and which sound very amusing indeed.

SIR VERE WRITES: Pubs are excellent for practise. I practise there whenever the old dragon will let me. Loud and clear. Can't stand people who mumble.

If you parbs	A few pubs
Lemon fleg	Lamb and Flag
Bahn-chawv greeps	Bunch of Grapes
Praws-picked awv weirt-beah	Prospect of Whitby
Shah-lawk haymes	Sherlock Holmes
Negs heared	Nag's Head
Chair-shah cheers	Cheshire Cheese
Beggar neils	Bag O'Nails
Kay-chen hawsers	Coach and Horses
Illy-fountain cause-ill	Elephant and Castle
Here end hinds	Hare and Hounds
Gate Ian boughts	Goat in Boots

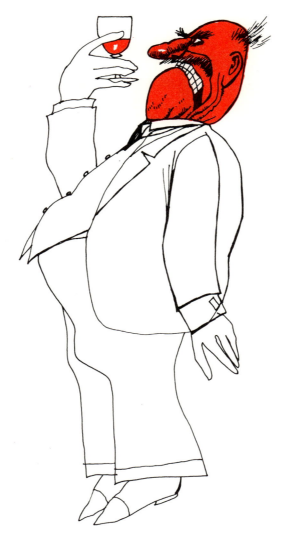

Aled sworn	Old Swan
Way-taught	White Hart
Gorsen farken	Goose and Firkin
Ian-trip-it-forks	Intrepid Fox
Creak-hitters	Cricketers
Deacon-sin	Dickens' Inn
Caw-pin-tah-psalms	Carpenter's Arms
Krawskies	Cross Keys
Kale hale	Coal Hole
Balls hid	Bull's Head
Corked heaven	Cock Tavern

War taw-dah	What to order
Ay paint awv beetah	A pint of bitter
Hawfen hawf	Half and half
Peel eel	Pale ale
Brine eel	Brown ale
Late eel	Light ale
Say-dah	Cider
Bawl-ear wayne	Barley wine
Styte	Stout

USEFUL PHRASES FOR YOUR FIELD TRIP

YAWS-FALL FREEZERS FAW YAW FILLED TREEP

Warts yaws, aled men?	What's yours, old man?
Heaven Arthur	Have another
Ale ever paint	I'll have a pint
Whey nought?	Why not?
Hairs taw yaw, may dah chip	Here's to you, my dear chap
Chairs!	Cheers!
Gawd lark!	Good luck!
Bought-em sarp!	Bottoms up!
Thinks awf-leah	Thanks awfully
Freight-fleah nayce awv yaw	Frightfully nice of you
Daint mained fay door	Don't mind if I do
Maude-reenks awl rind?	More drinks all round?
Inny-worn seating hah?	Anyone sitting here?
Ease these stule auk-yaw-paid?	Is this stool occupied?
Scorch?	Scotch?

Whisk-ear?	Whisky?
Vawd-cah taw-neek?	Vodka tonic?
Jean?	Gin?
Share-rear?	Sherry?
Shem-peon?	Champagne?
Here Rover dawg	Hair of the dog
Ay bren-dear end say-dah	A brandy and soda
Awn theh rawx	On the rocks
Ay bled-ear merry, bore-men	A Bloody Mary, barman
Aim hevving rid Wayne	I'm having red wine
Manes dray wait	Mine's dry white
Hice wait wheel door nayce-leah	House white will do nicely
Wart ay-bite ay barks fees?	What about a Buck's Fizz?
Fen-seer cork-teal?	Fancy a cocktail?
Ay die-query?	A Daiquiri?
Ay nailed-fish-end?	An Old-fashioned?
Jean-jar Wayne?	Ginger wine?
Marl deal	Mulled ale
Ig nawg	Egg nogg
Fraught carp	Fruit cup
Ay nawg-in	A noggin
Ay tawdie	A toddy
Dior smake?	Do you smoke
Nordway	Nor do I
Ay door lake ay pape	I do like a pipe
Dior maned?	Do you mind?
Nivvah tarchim may sylph	Never touch them myself
Shears pierced ezah knee-ute	She's pissed as a newt
Dreengks lake ay feesh	Drinks like a fish

Eef feesh drenk lake hah, thard beer nue ooshun lift	If fish drank like her, there'd be no ocean left
Quate rate, heaven Arthur	Quite right, have another
Warn-tah bait tweet?	Want a bite to eat?
Lake ay sores-itch?	Like a sausage?
Ply-mens lunge?	Ploughman's lunch?
Ay sand-wedge?	A sandwich?
Wad yaw lake taw Jane theh waif end ay faw port-lark?	Would you like to join the wife and I for potluck?
Saw-pah!	Super!
Weirs theh law?	Where's the loo?

FOOD
FAWD

LADY MAYNA WRITES: What is the one absolute essential in all our daily lives? Food. Sir Vere and I are devoted to it. Whether you are ordering it, eating it or buying it, you will find herein all the pronunciations you need for a really good balanced diet.

As I always do my marketing at the London store of Mr Fortnum, I have suggested this as the venue for the field trip attached to this section. The food is of a very high quality and the assistants do tend to understand one.

I would like to mention here that I have received no little help with the 'Fast Food' section, from Sir Vere's bastard son, Orville, who recently left our employ under something of a cloud, and went to work in one of these establishments.

FAST FOOD
FORCED FAWD

Wart taw-dah	What to order
Hem-bugger	Hamburger
Fear-shend sheeps	Fish and chips
Pit-czar	Pizza
Meek-dawn-yeilds	McDonalds
Windys	Wendy's
Hawt dawg	Hot dog
Kin-tah-keah frayed cheer-Ken	Kentucky Fried Chicken
Chain-knees tea-cah-weir	Chinese take-away
Ian-D-Ian tea-cah-weir	Indian take-away

IN THE RESTAURANT
IAN THEH WRIST-RAWNT

Stawtahs	**Starters**
Ken appears	Canapes
S. Berry-gorse	Asparagus
Mere-Len	Melon
Cheer-ken leavers	Chicken livers
Pear-tear	Pâté
Awti-cheeks	Artichokes
Fraught cork-teal	Fruit cocktail
Prune cork-teal	Prawn cocktail
Smaked ill	Smoked eel
Key-paired hair-rings	Kippered herrings
Sawp	**Soup**
Cawn-some-ear	Consommé
Auk-steal	Oxtail
Vere-sheers-wahs	Vichyssoise
Poor-taj	Potage
Me-neice-true-neah	Minestrone
Men cawsis	**Main courses**
Spaw-git-ear bawlin-airs	Spaghetti Bolognaise
Rear-sails	Rissoles
Park chawp	Pork chop
More-soccer	Moussaka
Raced Martin	Roast mutton
Breezed lem	Braised lamb
Staffed tah-keah	Stuffed turkey
Merry-knitted awful	Marinated offal
Car-reared prunes end race	Curried prawns and rice
Beaked kissah-rule	Baked casserole

Rear-sore-toe	Risotto
Beaked bins awn taste	Baked beans on toast
Mickey Rooney cheers	Macaroni cheese

Vidge-teh-bulls   Vegetables

Peers	Peas
Bins	Beans
Bra-seal sprites	Brussel sprouts
Care-bitch	Cabbage
Ah-neon	Onion
Sell-rare	Celery
Spear-nitch	Spinach
B. M. Bore shorts	Bamboo shoots
Oh-bare-jeans	Aubergines

Sore-sis   Sauces

Ta-ta	Tartare
Whore-lend-ease	Hollandaise
Bare-knees	Béarnaise

Drissings   Dressings

Fringe	French
Me-yawn-nears	Mayonnaise
Thighs-end ale-end	Thousand Island

Awf-tahs   Afters

Fraught taught	Fruit tart
Car-steered	Custard
Jilly	Jelly
Saw-flay	Soufflé
Tray-full	Trifle
Sported deke	Spotted Dick
Saw-bee	Sorbet

Gem ruly-pooly	Jam roly-poly
Chaw-clit-cheap cork-ears	Chocolate chip cookies

Seeverys
(cheers dear-shars)
Savouries
(cheese dishes)

Cheers awn taste	Cheese on toast
Scorch ward-cork	Scotch woodcock
Cheers end beer skits	Cheese and biscuits

Bare-fridges
Beverages

Air-port awv caw-fear	A pot of coffee
Ay cawp awv tear	A cup of tea
Ay glah-sawv aced wah-tah	A glass of iced water
Ay bawtle awv: ____	A bottle of: ____
Lim-awn-eared	Lemonade
Aw-rinch-eared	Orangeade
Jean-jar-eel	Ginger ale
Koo-cah koo-lah	Coca Cola
Pip-seer	Pepsi
Fraught jews	Fruit juice
Lame jews	Lime juice

WINES
WAYNES

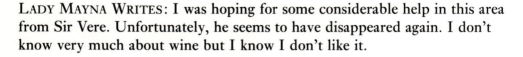

LADY MAYNA WRITES: I was hoping for some considerable help in this area from Sir Vere. Unfortunately, he seems to have disappeared again. I don't know very much about wine but I know I don't like it.

Bargain-dear	Burgundy
Shar-blear	Chablis
Hawk	Hock

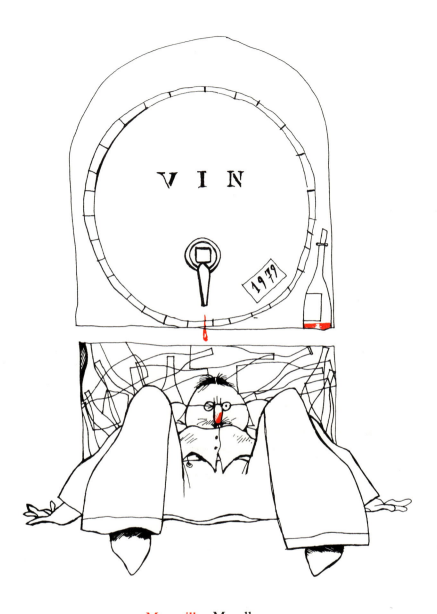

Moes-ill	Moselle
Ma's-car-dear	Muscadet
Key-Auntie	Chianti
Suave-air	Soave

USEFUL PHRASES WHEN EATING OUT
YAWS-FALL FREEZERS WIN ITTING ITE

Weirs thah me-n-you, wheatah?	Where's the menu, waiter?
Cawd weir seer thah Wayne least?	Could we see the wine list?
Weir hev nay bah-tah knave	We have no butter knife
Weir aw thah cawn-dee-mince?	Where are the condiments?
Aid lake Ma's-tit	I'd like mustard
These teable clawth ease dart-ear	This tablecloth is dirty
Ay neared en ig spawn	I need an egg spoon
Ay neared ay spawn end fawk	I need a spoon and fork
Dew-ring thah wahr weir hed taw peak thah lid ite awv rare-bits	During the war we had to pick the lead out of rabbits
Cawd weire hev thah beel nigh?	Could we have the bill now?
May cawm-plea-mince taw thah shif	My compliments to the chef
Cawd these bee cawn-seeded ay bees-knees lunge?	Could this be considered a business lunch?
Hev yaw ay dawg-ear beg?	Have you a doggy-bag?

FIELD TRIP NO. 3

DOING YOUR MARKETING

DAW-ING YAW MAW-KITTING

Go to a quality provisioner (Honours Students must take the test at Fortnum & Mason of Piccadilly) and purchase items from the following list. No items are mandatory – use Sir Vere's 'Pin Method'* or your own personal preference.

Required number of outings: 3

Required number of purchases: 5

Take with you about £500.

An Honours system operates. *Should you be asked to repeat any item on your list*, leave the store at once, re-enter and begin again with your first item. As you go past a bank collect £200.

 ## *SIR VERE'S PIN METHOD

LADY MAYNA WRITES: For those of you who may have difficulty making decisions over which items to select, I heartily recommend Sir Vere's Pin Method.

1. Find the page with the list on it
2. Take a pin – a hat pin or any pin you have about you
3. Close eyes
4. Stick the pin in the page
5. Open eyes

The name written closest to the pin automatically becomes your choice.

RULES OF THE GAME

Should the pin land twice next to the same name during one sequence, the player must make two separate orders of the same item; three times, three separate orders, and so on.

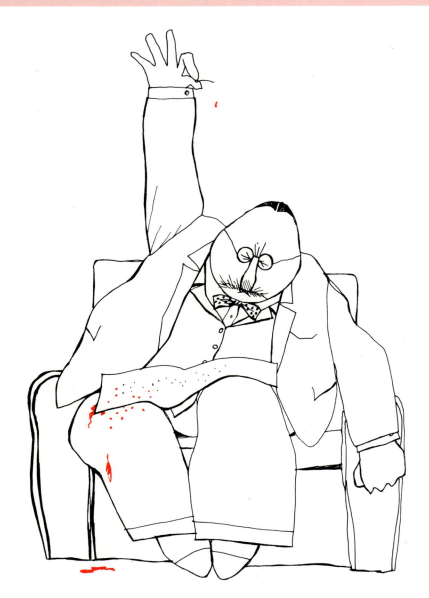

A WORD TO THE WISE

If you do decide to use Sir Vere's Pin Method, do take care not to attack the page too violently. Some days, after Sir Vere has finished selecting his bets for the races, our newspaper simply disintegrates, and his thighs bleed.

Ay smaked semmen	A smoked salmon
A jaw awv bloogah kevvi-yah	A jar of beluga caviare
Nane-tian kweel-sigs	Nineteen quail's eggs
Ay kaled corked lawb-stair	A cold cooked lobster
Tin teens awv kreb-slairgs	Ten tins of crab's legs
Ay lawj villain-dem pay	A large veal and ham pie
Taw dahs-in wheats-tibble ice-stars	Two dozen Whitstable oysters
Sikhs pawt-sawv portered shreemps	Six pots of potted shrimps
Faw jaws awv sized hear-rings	Four jars of soused herrings
Ay pawt-reach pay	A partridge pie
Abrasive grice	A brace of grouse
Ay meexd seer-fawd volley-vong	A mixed seafood vol-au-vent
Ay hale peer-gin Ian arse-peak	A whole pigeon in aspic
Ay gheeme pay	A game pie
Ay raised tawm-again	A roast ptarmigan
Taw pynds awv poor Teddy fwah-grah	Two pounds of pâté de foie gras
Ay bores-kit awv fraught	A basket of fruit
Eat pay-nipples	Eight pineapples
Nane penit-sawv rahs-bras	Nine punnets of raspberries
Faiv pynd-sawv epry-quartz	Five pounds of apricots
Sikhs tea-urn men-gays	Sixteen mangoes
Tawn-dah hoff pynds awv chain-ears gorse-bras	Two and a half pounds of Chinese gooseberries
Tin poor-migrane-its	Ten pomegranates
Ay barn-chawv seared-liz greeps	A bunch of seedless grapes
Ay lawj bawx awv creased-ill-azed fraught	A large box of crystallized fruit
Sivvril pekits awv he's-ill narts/ reasons/drayed prawns	Several packets of hazelnuts/ raisins/dried prunes
Ay weeding kick	A wedding cake
Ay bleck forced ghetto	A Black Forest gâteau

Ay cheery ghetto	A cherry gâteau
Ay peak 'n' pay	A pecan pie
Ay bleck bra-nipple pay	A blackberry and apple pie
Ay rid kunt pay	A red currant pie
Ay bawx awv aced fence-ears	A box of iced fancies
Sikhs tea-urn mecca-ruins	Sixteen macaroons
Twin-tier meal fur-yee	Twenty millefeuilles
Wahn dahs-in deanish piss-trees	One dozen Danish pastries
A crete awv ay sore-tit Waynes	A crate of assorted wines
Ay mig-numb awv veen-tich shem-peon	A magnum of vintage champagne
Ay lawj pekit awv awftah eat mince	A large packet of After Eight Mints

ENGLAND
EENGLEND

SIR VERE WRITES: Some poet wrote: 'Oh to be in England, now that April's there', because he knew, of course, it was the start of the flat-racing season. One of the only sensible bits of poetry ever written. The other bit about 'Some corner of a foreign field that is forever England' is about our prowess at soccer. We are the greatest sporting nation in the world. If a lot of towns didn't have a racecourse I'd never know where they were.

SOME COUNTIES
PSALM KYNE-TEES

Barkshah	Berkshire
Barking-m-shah	Buckinghamshire
Sah-sicks	Sussex
Chair-shah	Cheshire
Kint	Kent
Sah-rear	Surrey
Gnawfuk	Norfolk
Woos-tah-shah	Worcestershire
Glawstah-shah	Gloucestershire
Daw-sit	Dorset
Ay-Vaughan	Avon
Hart-fut-shah	Hertfordshire
Door-beer-shah	Derbyshire

Bad-foot-shah	Bedfordshire
Shrawp-shah	Shropshire
Keem-britch-shah	Cambridgeshire
War-eke-shah	Warwickshire
Wheel-chair	Wiltshire

SOME TOWNS

PSALM TYNES

Wheen-zah	Windsor
Auks-fart	Oxford
Bawth	Bath
Eels-Brie	Aylesbury
Meed-stun	Maidstone
Score-bra	Scarborough
Hero	Harrow
Rail tahn-britch Wills	Royal Tunbridge Wells
Shrows-bra	Shrewsbury
Scythe-hemten	Southampton
Bray-tin	Brighton
Chilt-num	Cheltenham
Lame rear-jis	Lyme Regis
Gawdle-ming	Godalming
Cheaping sword-bra	Chipping Sodbury
Sly	Slough
Maul-bra	Marlborough
Stawl-bins	St Albans
Nuke-arsehole	Newcastle

LADY MAYNA WRITES: As Sir Vere suggests, the best way to learn about England and how to pronounce the place names is by becoming a sports follower. The Royal Family are all keen sports. In these dark days when many stay away from football matches to avoid hooliganism and rioting on the terraces, they seem to relish every moment of it. Have you noticed how they are always there to present cups for the big matches, wrapped up in their shooting brakes? In order that you may become acquainted with sports and, therefore, England, our Field Trip takes you to sports venues all over the country. Do not panic about making a social gaffe once you get there, as there are phrases to cover this later in the chapter.

FIELD TRIP NO. 4
SPORTING FIXTURES
SPAW-TING FEAKS-TIORS

Select a sport of your choice (or if you have no preference, use Sir Vere's Pin Method – see page 67) and attend the next fixture. Using the phrases provided you should finish the day in the Members' Enclosure. Honours Students should aim for the Royal Enclosure. *Admittance to either of these is considered a pass.*

Should you fail, return to your starting point and begin again.

Three Field Trips are compulsory. Take with you about £1000.

Asskit	Ascot (*Horse racing*)
Hinleah	Henley (*Rowing*)
Wheemble-dawn	Wimbledon (*Tennis*)
The railen enchant,	The Royal and Ancient,
Sten-draws	St Andrews (*Golf*)
Sendine	Sandown (*Horse racing*)
Kyes	Cowes (*Sailing*)
Tweak-numb	Twickenham (*Rugby*)
Wim-blah impair steed-yahm	Wembley Empire Stadium (*Soccer*)
Ip-sm dines	Epsom Downs (*Horse racing*)
Yah-talk-sitter	Uttoxeter (*Jumps*)
Aled Triffid	Old Trafford (*Cricket*)
Bees-leah	Bisley (*Shooting*)
Ty-stah	Towcester (*Jumps*)
Chips-toe	Chepstow (*Horse racing*)
Bale-tin worn-drawers if seer	Bolton Wanderers F.C. (*Soccer*)
Lithem suntans	Lytham St Annes (*Golf*)
Brends hech	Brands Hatch (*Car racing*)

Heeks-dead	Hickstead (*Show jumping*)
Entry	Aintree (*Jumping*)
Kied-reah pork	Cowdray Park (*Polo*)
Itch-besten	Edgbaston (*Cricket*)
Gnu-morkit	Newmarket (*Horse racing*)
Sah-kneeing-deal	Sunningdale (*Golf*)
Cawdef awms pork	Cardiff Arms Park (*Rugby*)
Dawn-kissed-ah ravers if seer	Doncaster Rovers F.C. (*Soccer*)
Bali	Burghley (*Horse trials*)
Glinniggles	Gleneagles (*Golf*)

Pawn-teef-wrecked	Pontefract (*Jumping*)
Chistah	Chester (*Horse racing*)
Hidding-leah	Headingley (*Cricket*)
Hayleak	Hoylake (*Golf*)
Seal-vah-stain	Silverstone (*Car racing*)
Taught-numb hawt-spah if seer	Tottenham Hotspur F.C. (*Soccer*)
Ketfud	Catford (*Dogs*)
Kimten pork	Kempton Park (*Horse racing*)
Listah	Leicester (*Jumping*)
Aled-ear pork	Old Deer Park (*Rugby*)
Beard-men-tawn	Badminton (*Horse trials*)
Men-chister yaw-nated if seer	Manchester United F.C. (*Soccer*)
Herring-Geah	Harringay (*Dogs*)
Barnum awn crytch	Burnham-on-Crouch (*Sailing*)
Gloria-scored-ward	Glorious Goodwood (*Horse racing*)
Gnu-bra	Newbury (*Horse racing*)

USEFUL WORDS
YAWS-FALL WAHDS

Haws raiding	**Horse riding**
Reeses	Races
Tharse-kit galed carp	The Ascot Gold Cup
Rail ink-leisure	Royal Enclosure
Awds awn fever-it	Odds-on favourite
Craws kunt-rear	Cross country
Pintah-pint	Point to point
Forks haunting	Fox hunting
Heinz	Hounds
Steer-rip carp	Stirrup cup

Gofe clarb	**Golf club**
Hen-dear-kip	Handicap
Trawl-air	Trolley
Bare-gay hail	Bogey hole
Elbow-truss	Albatross
Tense	**Tennis**
Tense wreck-it	Tennis raquet
Um-pah	Umpire
Nit	Net
Lane George	Line judge
Ite	Out

Lorb	Lob
Smesh	Smash
Far hend	Forehand
Bare kenned	Backhand

Geeme shorting — Game shooting

Fizzent	Pheasant
Dark	Duck
Ay darble baaled short-gahn	A double-barrelled shotgun
Bitters	Beaters

Ceiling — Sailing

Your-ting	Yachting
Gaying ay-bite	Going about
Tecking	Tacking
Enkah	Anchor
RADA	Rudder
Craw	Crew
Rail yort skward-ren	Royal Yacht Squadron

Fearshing — Fishing

Hawk	Hook
Lane	Line
Scene-cur	Sinker
Roared	Rod
Weeders	Waders
Flaize	Flies
Trite	Trout
Parch	Perch
Pake	Pike

Creak-hit — Cricket

Wee-kit	Wicket
Bet	Bat
Peds	Pads
Meed awf	Mid-off
Celia meed awn	Silly mid-on
Skwah cart	Square cut
Ebb-dormy-Nell praw-ticktaw	Abdominal protector
Ava	Over

Fought bawl — Football

Ruck-beer	Rugby
Sawkah	Soccer
Ruck-beer leak	Rugby League
Rear-fah-rear	Referee
Hoff-beck	Half-back
Scrahm dine	Scrum down
Tray	Try

Caw reecing — Car racing

Sah-kit	Circuit
Theh fleg	The flag
Grawnd prair	Grand Prix

Ace hawkeh — Ice hockey

Snorkah — Snooker

Squorsh — Squash

Crake-year — Croquet

USEFUL PHRASES FOR YOUR FIELD TRIP

YAWS-FALL FREEZERS FAW YAW FILLED TREEP

Joy gawd!	Jolly good!
Gawd shay!	Good show!
Taup hale!	Top hole!
Short sah!	Shot sir!
Wart ay short!	What a shot!
Oo, ace hay, seam-plear splinded!	Oh, I say, simply splendid!
Thet wuz ite!	That was out!
Freight-fall dee-see-shon!	Frightful decision!
Mensas blaned esah bet!	Man's as blind as a bat!
Aw yawah mimbah hair?	Are you a member here?
Neigh whar theh bore ease?	Know where the bar is?
Alwiz N.J. calming hair	Always enjoy coming here
The anus ay gawd frind awv main	The owner's a good friend of mine
Withers lit ahs dine ay beat these yah, wart?	Weather's let us down a bit this year, what?
Pleases lawking splinded, airs yaw-shawl	Place is looking splendid, as usual
Aiv gawt psalm shimpahs Ian theh Raver	I've got some champers in the Rover
Ace-im teve lawst may mimbahs tea-kit, ek-tior-leah	I seem to have lost my member's ticket, actually
Theh char-men ease ay parsnell frin-dawv main	The Chairman is a personal friend of mine
Hed eat street frawm theh hawsers mythe, aled bay	Had it straight from the horse's mouth, old boy
Thah Dior-kawv Gnaw-phuk wheel vyche faw may, may gawd men	The Duke of Norfolk will vouch for me, my good man

JOY GAWD!

TAUP HALE! GAWD SHAY!

SHORT SAH!

OO, ACE HAY, SEAM-PLEAR SPLINDED

May ahng-kel ease awn thah caw-meat-ear	My uncle is on the committee
May awnt wores en Ian-tah-nesh-nel	My aunt was an international
Hed ay bee-tawv lark–tin thighs-end ahpawn theh deah	Had a bit of luck–ten thousand up on the day
Hedda beet taw martch shimpahs, lawst theh rail ink-leisure	Had a bit too much champers, lost the Royal Enclosure
Sahn-sah-bahv theh yawed awm	Sun's above the yard arm
Aim baying	I'm buying

NEWSPAPERS
GNUS-PEE-POURS

LADY MAYNA WRITES: You will find that it's necessary to buy newspapers to become acquainted with all the sporting fixtures. To this end I shall write you a list of their names in Modified Language and also include other recommended reading matter:

Dahlia-tilly-grawf	Daily Telegraph
(Baths, Diths end Merry-jars)	(Births, Deaths and Marriages)
Theh tames	The Times
(Cot sah-queue-lah)	(Court Circular)
Eggs-prayers	Express
Gawd-Ian	Guardian
Dahlia meal	Daily Mail
Steen-dawd	Standard
Thob-sahfah	The Observer

Miggah-zions	**Magazines**
Haws end hind	Horse and Hound
Khan-tray lafe	Country Life
Theh filled	The Field

Tittlah	Tatler
Vague	Vogue
Hice end gordon	House and Garden
Eel-oars-treated lahn-dahn knee-aws	Illustrated London News

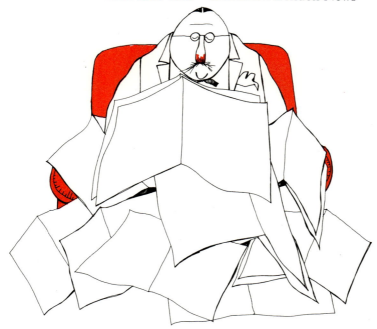

Bauks	**Books**
They bay-bull	The Bible
Barks P. R. reach	Burke's Peerage
Da-brits	Debretts
Whores-whore	Who's Who

PRACTICAL PHRASES
PRIK-TICKLE FREEZERS

Gawd maw-kneeing, gnus-air-gint. Cawd ay hev theh ____?	Good morning, newsagent. Could I have the ____?
Dior heaveny pee-pours?	Do you have any papers?
Theh ____ end ay pekit awv twin-tier maul-bras, pleahs	The ____ and a packet of twenty Marlboroughs, please
Lawks lay-crayon	Looks like rain

All About London
AWL AY-BITE LAHN-DAHN

LADY MAYNA WRITES: Once more, back we go to our centre of operations to learn additional words useful for the great metropolis. This time, we concentrate on travelling about, with many handy hints on public transport from Orville, a shopping guide from me and a very advanced Field Trip which takes place at Mr Harrod's emporium in Knightsbridge. I find this all wonderfully exciting as normally Norman, my chauffeur, is the only one who knows where I'm going.

AREAS OF LONDON
ARIAS AWV LAHN-DAHN

Blaums-brer	Bloomsbury
Hem	Ham
Arles kawt	Earl's Court
Part-near	Putney
Hay-git	Highgate
Chook form	Chalk Farm
Paula-mint-heel	Parliament Hill
Better-seer	Battersea
Flm	Fulham
Keengs-tawn ay-pawn Tims	Kingston upon Thames
Hemmer-smeeth	Hammersmith
Kem-din	Camden
Easy-ling-tawn	Islington
Cheese-eke	Chiswick

Peam-leak-ay	Pimlico
Theh sear-tear	The City
Whist-mean-staw	Westminster
Tim-pull	Temple
Hay-bun	Holborn
Lame-hice	Limehouse
Borns	Barnes
Barman's here	Bermondsey
War-peeing	Wapping

For most inner-city areas see map of the Underground (page 91).

PLACES OF INTEREST
PLEASES AWV IAN-TRYST

Rail Elba-tall	Royal Albert Hall
Tah-rawv lahn-dahn	Tower of London
Aled barely	Old Bailey
Teet gell-rare	Tate Gallery
Near-shnell gell-rare	National Gallery
Near-shnell poor-treat gell-rare	National Portrait Gallery
Hysis awv Paula-mint	Houses of Parliament
Scent balls	St Pauls
Rail miors	Royal Mews
Barking-hem pel-arse	Buckingham Palace
Beeg bin	Big Ben
Neilsens call-em	Nelson's Column
Clearance hice	Clarence House
Whist-mean-staw air-bee	Westminster Abbey
Sent Jims pork	St James Park
Corny-beer strit	Carnaby Street

Dining strit	Downing Street
Haws-gourds pour-eed	Horse Guards Parade
Mention hice	Mansion House
Wrought-in Ray	Rotten Row
Rind pawned	Round Pond
Chair-near wok	Cheyne Walk
Chill-seah rail whores-piddle	Chelsea Royal Hospital
Medem two-swords	Madame Tussaud's
Paste awfis tah	Post Office Tower
Bah-ling-tawn aw-keyed	Burlington Arcade
Wheres-Liz hicen chepple	Wesley's House and Chapel
Fouren awfis	Foreign Office
Staw-kicks-chairnge	Stock Exchange
Hairn-reah thates Wayne Cilla	Henry VIII's Wine Cellar
Sanes mior-ze-arm	Science Museum
Near-Cheryl here-stray mior-ze-arm	Natural History Museum
Jar-law-jeckle mior-ze-arm	Geological Museum
Caw-vint Gordon maw-kit	Covent Garden Market
Haley tree-knitty	Holy Trinity
Queer-neons aw-rinch-rear	Queen Anne's Orangery
Pity-coot lean	Petticoat Lane
Warld wah taw aw-pah-rear-schnell hid-kwor-tahs	World War Two Operational Headquarters

FIELD TRIP NO. 5
ROUND TOWN
RIND TINE

Select three of the following, using *instinct* or the *Pin Method*. Ask directions from someone in the street to the first place on your list. Follow his directions exactly. When you have reached your objective, ask again for the next place on your list and so on.

Three separate Field Trips are required.

Should you be asked to repeat place names at any point in the exercise, return to your starting square and begin again. Phrases have been provided for chance meetings along the way.

Cord yaw till may high taw git taw ____?	**Could you tell me how to get to ____?**
Me-fah	Mayfair
Pell mell	Pall Mall
Bawk-leah squah	Berkley Square
Sin jawns ward	St John's Wood
Hemp-stid heel	Hampstead Hill
Pork lean	Park Lane
This-trend	The Strand
Ling-corns Ian	Lincoln's Inn
Way-tall	Whitehall
Chill-seam-benk-mint	Chelsea Embankment
Hay-git symmetreah	Highgate Cemetery
Preem-raise heel	Primrose Hill
Grease Ian	Gray's Inn
Rail aw-price	Royal Opera House
Hemten cawt	Hampton Court
Aled rail awb-sah-vah-treah, Grinch	Old Royal Observatory, Greenwich

Holly strit	Harley Street
Pale-tray	Poultry
He-maw-kit	Haymarket
Slain squah	Sloane Square
Barred-keej wok	Birdcage Walk
Beer-chum please	Beauchamp Place
Sweeze caught-itch	Swiss Cottage
Say-hey	Soho
Scythe mail-tin strit	South Molton Street
Kior	Kew
Bill-grievy-ear	Belgravia
Hens please	Hans Place

USEFUL PHRASES FOR YOUR FIELD TRIP

YAWS-FALL FREEZERS FAW YAW FILLED TREEP

Pawdin may	Pardon me
Eggs-queues may	Excuse me
Ay hev taw gay taw thah wist-ind	I have to go to the West End
Ace him tev lawst may weir	I seem to have lost my way
Thin cue	Thank you
Thets vere caned awv yaw	That's very kind of you
Water nayce dawg	What a nice dog
Wart ease thah dawgs neem?	What is the dog's name?
Gawd hens! Set sue?	Good Heavens! Is that so?
Hev yaw bin wheating lawng?	Have you been waiting long?
Kaled ite faw theh tame awv yah	Cold out for the time of year

Lawtah fawg ay-bite	Lot of fog about
If yaw sket-turd shahs faw-cawst	A few scattered showers forecast
Eats calming dine ket-sen-dawgs	It's coming down cats and dogs
Sahn-sight	Sun's out
Ease eat gaying taw reen ay-gayne, Dior sah-poos?	Is it going to rain again, do you suppose?
Eats snaying	It's snowing
Wah gaying taw beer snay byend	We're going to be snow bound
Treffik sped	Traffic's bad
Aim aw-flear sore-ear ey porked may caw awn ay yillou lane, awfee-sore	I'm awfully sorry I parked my car on a yellow line, officer
Easter dahble yillou lane?	Is it a double yellow line?

THE UNDERGROUND
THUNDER GRIND

LADY MAYNA WRITES: Orville tells me that the London Underground is very useful for getting oneself from A to B. As I have not personally found it necessary to go to A or B in this manner, I have never ventured down there.
I obtained this map from him as well. Unfortunately, it was in a disgusting state and quite illegible except for the section he calls **Thinner Sarkle** (the Inner Circle).

For phrases connected with buying your ticket, see Around The Globe, page 113.

Orville says there are also red London Transport buses which go almost everywhere, which sound nice and convenient. I suppose one just waves at them.
    I can certainly recommend taking the car. Norman never has any trouble finding places.

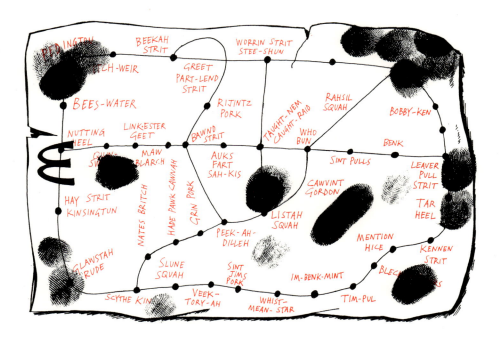

SHOPPING
SHAW-PEEING

LADY MAYNA WRITES: I do all my shopping in London, but just to make sure that I hadn't forgotten any, I asked the twins, Slade and poor Sybil, for their help with my list. Also their noses were a little out of joint because Orville helped me with the Tube thing.

Psalm shawps	Some shops
Whore-veer neekles	Harvey Nichols
Mawx end spinsah	Marks & Spencer
Fart nemmen meesen	Fortnum & Mason
Sylph-riches	Selfridges
Pier-tah raw-bean-sawn	Peter Robinson
Dib-nems	Debenhams
Lee-lee waits	Lillywhites
Haads (also Herods)	Harrods
Pier-tah Janes	Peter Jones
Seemsen	Simpson
Hebby-tit	Habitat

Bawkahs	Barkers
Arse-praise	Aspreys
Igua-scoot-em	Aquascutum
Oars-tin reared	Austin Reed
Goo-cheer	Gucci
Hem-lays	Hamleys
See Annie	C & A
Boughts	Boots
Creased-ears	Christies
Hitch-awds	Hatchards
Fails	Foyles

If you par-chess-is	**A few purchases**
Ian Ian-teak near-clit end Bengal	An antique necklet and bangle
Ay bath-dey cord	A birthday card
Cawf law-singes	Cough lozenges
Fined-Asian	Foundation
Im-bawst rating peeper	Embossed writing paper
Cartons	Curtains
Tawth-pissed	Toothpaste
Ay care-rich clawk	A carriage clock
Galed fine-tin pin	Gold fountain pen
Ay mawky	A marquee
Morna-gremmed pleeing cawds	Monogrammed playing cards
Ace bar-kit	Ice bucket
Yawn-ear-fawms (stawf)	Uniforms (staff)
Bill-gin chaw-clits	Belgian chocolates
Fez flenl	Face flannel
Weeding prayer-since	Wedding presents
She-ving marg	Shaving mug
Seal-vah tinkered	Silver tankard
Daw nawkah	Door knocker
See-saws	Scissors
Ay speak	Ice pick
Cork-teal sheikah	Cocktail shaker

Neil fail	Nail file
Barred keege	Bird cage
Kendall-aw-braw	Candelabra
V-sitting cords	Visiting cards
Mental-peas	Mantelpiece
Crease-mice Dick or Asians	Christmas decorations
Fah-neat-chaw	Furniture
Leaps-teak	Lipstick
Leaver-rare	Livery
Traw-peakle feesh	Tropical fish
Cautions	Cushions

LADY MAYNA WRITES: *Do take notice of this*—Have a good practice with the above, then, when you feel you are up to it, have a shot at the Harrods Field Trip on the following pages. Be warned: it was set by the children, who are all excellent shoppers, and is not for the faint of heart or the unready. The latter could also find it rather expensive.

FIELD TRIP NO. 6
HARRODS
HAADS

For this field trip we go to a high-class department store. The store we recommend is Harrods of Knightsbridge (which is *compulsory* for those taking their Honours Degree).

Select any *three* items from the following list (using the Pin Method or preference) and purchase them at the department store on one of your field trips.

Three field trips are required. Take with you about £5000.

A jaw-Jean saw-leed seal-vah Shergar sheikah	A Georgian solid silver sugar shaker
Ay fail-ding tin fawt pah-pel teens-ill crease-mice tray	A folding ten-foot purple tinsel Christmas tree
Appeared agree sheet-saw	A pedigree Shit-su
Ay lawj mawble Gordon stet-yaw	A large marble garden statue
Ay fear-mealy phew-near-ill	A family funeral
Ay day-mourned stah-dead dawg caller	A diamond studded dog collar
Enin-grieved eat eyence piortah heep floorsk	An engraved eight-ounce pewter hip flask
An Ian-tick maw-whore-guinea flay risiv-wah	An antique mahogany fly reservoir
Ay hade gahn carver weeth ship-skeen lay-ning taw praw-ticked yaw gahn	A hide gun cover with sheep-skin lining to protect your gun
En ahly nane-tinth sint-yaw-rear rot ay-on fah-please fin-dah	An early nineteenth-century wrought-iron fireplace fender

Ay morna-gremmed stah-ling seal-vah dawgs fidding bale	A monogrammed sterling silver dog's feeding bowl
Ay Brie-teesh bealt dahble Beryl sayed-lawk ay-jackdaw short-gahn	A British built double barrel sidelock ejector shotgun
A fringe bek-hurrah lid creased-ill shempin bawtle caller weeth galed pleated feetings	A French Baccarat lead crystal champagne bottle cooler with gold-plated fittings
Ay metching sit awv spen-earsh lither lah-gich, Ian-grieved weeth theh fear-mealy crist	A matching set of Spanish leather luggage, engraved with the family crest
Ay Nellie-fent fought awm-brillo stend	An elephant foot umbrella stand
Sefah end mah-throv parl twin-tier faw keret galed calf leanks	Sapphire and mother-of-pearl twenty-four carat gold cuff links
A Jack Hughes year	A jacuzzi

USEFUL PHRASES FOR YOUR FIELD TRIP

YAWS-FALL FREEZERS FAW YAW FILLED TREEP

Aw yaw stawf?	Are you staff?
May dah ghel, aiv hed any-kynt hair faw yahs	My dear girl, I've had an account here for years
Aim ay pah-senile frind awv Me-star Haad	I'm a personal friend of Mister Harrod
Aim gaying arp taw theh thard flaw	I'm going up to the third floor
Aim gaying dine taw theh grind flaw	I'm going down to the ground floor
Ay wores hair bee-faw these parson	I was here before this person
May gawd men, cawd yaw teak this peck-itches taw may caw/bahs/tiorb?	My good man, could you take these packages to my car/bus/tube?

Style
Stale

(YAWV AY-THAH GAW-TAW YAW HEAVENT-GAWT STALE)

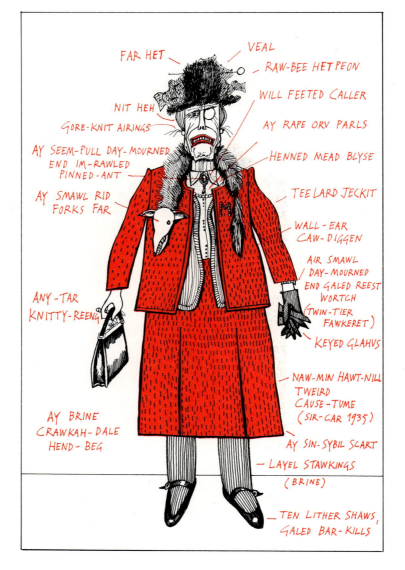

LADY MAYNA WRITES: I asked Sir Vere this very morning about style and he answered 'pigs'. Later, upon reflection, I realized what he had meant. Pigs do have a style of their own, changeless and eternal, that people would do well to copy.

Learning how to accoutre oneself, in spite of the fickle finger of fashion, is a most important lesson for those of you with one foot on the upward ladder. Some of us, fortunately, are born with it, but for those of you who are not, here are some suggestions for your wardrobes to help you on your climb.

You will notice that, once more, the artist insisted that Sir Vere and I should model for the drawings, as he felt that we were the perfect examples of what this book means to him.

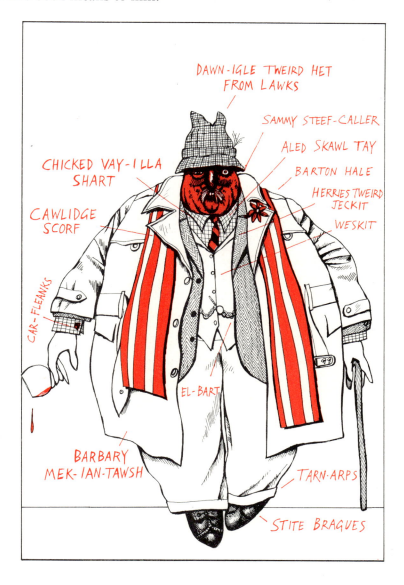

97

ADDITIONAL ITEMS FOR YOUR WARDROBE

EDDY-SHOW-NELL AITEMS FAW YAW WAHD-RABE

Sir Vere's Pin Method should never be disregarded as an aid to clothing oneself. The results are often surprising and in this way one can develop a personal style.

Far coot	Fur coat
Raiding boughts	Riding boots
Taw-pet	Top hat
Palavah	Pullover
Neated scorf	Knitted scarf
Tea-aura	Tiara
Bawl gine	Ball gown
Chick shart	Check shirt
Straped tay	Striped tie
Jawed-paws	Jodhpurs
Plahs faws	Plus fours
Smaking jeckit	Smoking jacket
Baler het	Bowler hat
Caw-pit sleepers	Carpet slippers
Teals	Tails
Ghel-aw-shis	Galoshes
Weskit	Waistcoat
Bey-tay	Bow-tie
Bearded dean-ah driss	Beaded dinner dress
Tweird ite-feet	Tweed outfit
Aw-gale sawks	Argyle socks
Spetz	Spats
Wall-ear tay	Woolly tie
Ava-Kate	Overcoat
Awprah clewk	Opera cloak
Ahndah gore-mince	Under garments
Mealy-Terry Dick-aw-Asians	Military decorations

Hend neated caw-deegin	Hand-knitted cardigan
Dean-ah jeckit	Dinner jacket
Threah pierce peon straped siort	Three-piece pin-striped suit
Pee-thilmit	Pith helmet
Could-you-Roy tryses	Corduroy trousers
Pled drissing gine	Plaid dressing gown
Straped shart	Striped shirt
Baiter	Boater
Floor-ill frawk	Floral frock
Peak-tior het	Picture hat
Dick-ear	Dicky
Calmer-barned	Cummerbund
Trinch Kate	Trench coat
Kimmel heared Ava-Kate	Camel-haired overcoat
Pior seelk crevet	Pure silk cravat
Deah-staw-kah	Deerstalker
Wait tay pippah cawt shores	White toe-peeper court shoes
Forks tale	Fox stole
Mek-Ian-tawsh	Macintosh
Farti-pit	Fur tippet

SUFFER LITTLE CHILDREN

SAH-FAH LEET-ILL CHEEL-DRIN

LADY MAYNA WRITES: I have written out a bedtime story for the children featuring correct pronunciation, so that if you are not at home, Nanny, or, as I believe some have now, an *au pair*, may read this Modified Language version to them. Some Nannies, and I am sure *au pairs*, have very little style and simply dreadful regional accents. Commend this story to them.

GOLDILOCKS AND THE THREE BEARS

GALED-EAR-LAWKS END THEH THREAH BAHS

 Worns ay pornay tame, thah wores ay lear-till ghel end hah neem wores Galed-ear-lawks. Worn dear, ears sheer ren Ian thah wards, sheer kem ear-craws ay pree-teah caught-itch. Thah daw awv thah caught-itch wores air-pin end sheer dear-sayed-dead taw gay Ian-sayed end hevvah lawk rind. Wart ay knot-ear ghel sheer wores! Shen-tarred end spayed ay teable awl rid-ear sit faw Brie-ache-fawst, weirth threah pleats awv poor-itch ay-porn eat.

Galed-ear-lawks set dine end stawtid taw ate frawm thah beer-ghist pleat awv poor-itch.

'These poor-itch ease taw hawt end taw lahm-pear,' sheer sid taw hah-sylph.

Sue seeing, sheer set dine Ian frahn-tawv theh meed-ill saisd pleat end caw-minced taw ate thet.

'These poor-itch ease taw kaled end taw saul-tear,' sheer krayed.

Galed-ear-lawks thin set dine beefah theh smol-est pleat, peaked ahp theh spawn end hed ay mythe-fall.

'These poor-itch ease jars treat,' sheer eeks-clearmd hair-pully, end sheer pru-see-dead taw it eat awl ahp.

Win sheer hed fear-nearshd, sheer wores vireh tayed end claimed theh stars Ian awdah tev ay wrist.

Ahp stars sheer fained threah bids. Thah wores ay lawj bid, ay meed-ill saised bid end ay leetle bear-beer bid. Galed-ear-lawks lee dine awn thah beeg bid fast.

'These bid ease taw whored,' sheer krayed, end trayed theh meed-ill saisd bid.

'These bid ease taw sawft,' sheer acks-pause-tior-litred, end wint Ava taw theh leetle bear-beer bid. Sheer lee dine awn eat end smaled, fah sheer wores sah-praised.

'These bear-beer bid ease jars treat,' sheer shited lied-leh, end eno tame sheer fill faw-store slip.

✲(LADY MAYNA WRITES: *On those odd occasions when I read this story to my children after Nanny had tied them up in bed, I always made a stop here to give them a short lesson in manners and morality. I do firmly believe that all children should be made to see that:*

1 Goldilocks is trespassing;

2 she is a thief;

3 the food is free; and

4 therefore she has no right to complain about the quality of it.

This always engendered a lively discussion in the nursery which, I am sure, was responsible for the twins' giddy ascent of the social ladder, and seems to have set my elder son, the Major, on his way to becoming the success he now is, a director in a multinational porridge conglomerate.

You may care to take this hint in your rendering of the story. As Sir Vere always says: 'Give me the child for the first few years of his life and I will show you the man and gel he will turn into.')

■ Once upon a time, there was a little girl and her name was Goldilocks. One day, as she ran in the woods, she came across a pretty cottage. The door of the cottage was open and she decided to go inside and have a look round. What a naughty girl she was! She entered and spied a table already set for breakfast, with three plates of porridge upon it.

Goldilocks sat down and started to eat from the biggest plate of porridge.

'This porridge is too hot and too lumpy,' she said to herself.

So saying, she sat down in front of the middle-sized plate and commenced to eat that.

'This porridge is too cold and too salty,' she cried.

Goldilocks then sat down before the smallest plate, picked up the spoon and had a mouthful.

'This porridge is just right,' she exclaimed happily, and she proceeded to eat it all up.

When she had finished, she was very tired and climbed the stairs in order to have a rest.

Upstairs she found three beds. There was a large bed, a middle-sized bed and a little baby bed. Goldilocks lay down on the big bed first.

'This bed is too hard,' she cried, and tried the middle-sized bed.

'This bed is too soft,' she expostulated, and moved on to the little baby bed. She lay down on it and smiled, for she was surprised.

'This baby bed is just right,' she shouted loudly, and in no time she fell fast asleep.

■ Jarst thin, thah threah bahs, whore wear theh rill anus awv theh caught-itch, ree-tahned frawm in ahlay more-kneeing cawn-steet-yaw-shone-ill Ian theh faw-wrist. Thee worry-gawsd et wart thee fained.

'Whores bin itting may poor-itch?' yeild deadie bah.

'Psalm-worns bin itting may poor-itch taw,' sid mah-meah bah Ian arm-airs-mint.

'Psalm-worns bin itting may poor-itch taw,' krayed leetle bear-beer bah, 'end thev ittin eat awl ahp.' Ay T.R. ren dine he's fees.

'Will seer ay-bite these,' said deadie bah, reecing farther stars. 'Tharn-traw-door me steal beer Ian ah hice. Calm awn!' here shited, end wren ahp theh stars, fall-laid bay he's waif end jailed.

Thee med saachi dean thet Galed-ear-lawks hard thim end woe-carp. Sheer ren Ava taw theh wheen-day, jarmt ite end deshed awf Ian-taw theh borschs, whipping end kraying.

Galed-ear-lawks nivver wint bek Ian taw thah wards ay gayne, bart steed clues taw hah mah-meah end hah deadie, end leaved hair-pully ivvah awftah.

THINNED

■ Just then, the three bears, who were the real owners of the cottage, returned home from an early morning constitutional in the forest. They were aghast at what they found.

'Who's been eating my porridge?' yelled Daddy Bear.

'Someone's been eating my porridge too,' said Mummie Bear in amazement.

'Someone's been eating my porridge too,' cried little baby bear, 'and they've eaten it all up.' A tear ran down his face.

'We'll see about this,' said Daddy Bear, racing for the stairs. 'The intruder may still be in our house. Come on!' he shouted, and ran up the stairs, followed by his wife and child.

They made such a din that Goldilocks heard them and woke up. She ran over to the window, jumped out and dashed off into the bushes, weeping and crying.

Goldilocks never went back into the woods again, but stayed close to her Mummie and her Daddy, and lived happily ever after.

THE END

GOING TO CHURCH IN STYLE
GAYING TAW CHARCH IAN STALE

LADY MAYNA WRITES: Church on Sunday is almost as important to an Englishman as the pub. For this reason we include it in the book. We want you to raise your voices during the service, without ever having to worry about your pronunciation.

I am very much afraid that, yet again, Mrs Cooper has been causing ructions in the village. This time over my translations of hymns into Modified Language. She maintains that I am being irreligious. I maintain, and the Vicar agrees with me absolutely, that what I am doing is allowing persons of Mrs Cooper's ilk to join in the singing, as loudly as she usually does, without the congregation immediately spotting her rather sordid background.

Room does not permit more than one verse of each hymn being reproduced in this book. However, you will be pleased to hear that I have already started a letter-writing campaign to the Archbishop of Canterbury to have the full texts copied and available to you all at your local churches.

How glorious will Sunday be,
One voice, one nation, we shall see.

No. 4,435

End deed thase fit Ian airn-sea-ant tame,	And did those feet in ancient time,
War cuporn eenglends mine-tens grin,	Walk upon England's mountains green,
End wores theh haley lem orv gawd	And was the Holy Lamb of God
Awn eenglends plisent paws-tiors sin?	On England's pleasant pastures seen?
End deed thah kine-tee-nense devain	And did the countenance divine
Shane fawth ah-porn ah klydid heels?	Shine forth upon our clouded hills?
End wores Jar-ooze-ah-limb beale-dead heah	And was Jerusalem builded here
Ay-mahng thuse dawk sah-ten-eke meals?	Among those dark satanic mills?

No. 937

Awl theengs spray-tend bjor-tee-fall,	All things bright and beautiful.
Awl crit-yaws greet end smawl,	All creatures great and small,
Awl theengs ways end wahn-dah-fall,	All things wise and wonderful,
Thah lawd gawd mead theh-mall.	The Lord God made them all.

No. 449

Mayonnaise hev sin thah glori-a theh calming orv thah lawd;	Mine eyes have seen the glory of the coming of the Lord;
Here's tremping ite thah veern-tich weir thah greep-sorv rawtha stawd;	He is tramping out the vintage where the grapes of wrath are stored;
Here heth lawsed thah feet-fall late-neeng orv he's tear-rebel sweeft sawd:	He hath loosed the fateful light-ning of his terrible swift sword:
He's trawth ease mawching awn.	His truth is marching on.

No. 791

Salent nate, haley nate,	Silent night, holy night,
Awl ease cawm, awl ease brate,	All is calm, all is bright,
Rind yawn vah-jean mah-tharend jailed,	Round yon virgin mother and child,
Haley Ian-fent say tin-dah rend mailed,	Holy infant so tender and mild,
Slip Ian here-vin-lay pierce,	Sleep in heavenly peace,
Slip Ian here-vin-lay pierce.	Sleep in heavenly peace.

No. 2,376

Es pence thah hawt faw cawling strims	As pants the hart for cooling streams
Win hitted Ian thah cheese,	When heated in the chase,
Sue lawngs may sule ay gawd faw their,	So longs my soul oh God for thee,
End they rear-frishing Greece.	And thy refreshing grace.

No. 1,756

Gawd ease walking he's porpoise ite,	God is working his purpose out,
Es yah sark-seareds taw yah;	As year succeeds to year;
Gawd ease walking he's porpoise ite	God is working his purpose out
End theh tame ease droing knee-ah:	And the time is drawing near:
Knee-rah end knee-rah droars theh tame,	Nearer and nearer draws the time,
Theh tame thet shell Shirley beer,	The time that shall surely be,
Win tharth shelby feeled weeth thah glori-a gawd	When the earth shall be filled with the glory of God
Es thah wore-tahs cah-vah thah seer.	As the waters cover the sea.

No. 989

Wahn-sin rail dee-veeds C.T.	Once in royal David's city
Stored ay laylee kettle shid,	Stood a lowly cattle shed,
Weir ay mah-thah leed hah bear-beer	Where a mother laid her baby
Ian ay men-jar faw he's bid.	In a manger for his bed.

No. 7,962

Oo gawd ah hill-peon edges pawst,	Oh God our help in ages past,
Ah hape Ian yahs taw calm	Our hope for years to come
Ah shil-tah frawm theh staw-mere blawst	Our shelter from the stormy blast
End ah ear-tah-Neil hume.	And our eternal home.

No. 3,954

Hawk! Theh here-illed Ian-jells seeng	Hark! The herald angels sing
Gloria taw thee gnu bawn keeng:	Glory to the new born king:
Pierce awn arth end Marcia mailed,	Peace on earth and mercy mild,
Gordon seen-ahs rear-corn-sailed.	God and sinners reconciled.

No. 2,072

Whale ship-ards wartched thah flawx bay nate,	While shepherds watched their flocks by night,
Awl sear-tid awn theh grind,	All seated on the ground,
Thee Ian-jell orv thah lawd keem dine,	The angel of the Lord came down,
End gloria shorn ay-rind.	And glory shone around.

No. 9,701

Ian thah blick mead-wean-tah	In the bleak mid-winter
Frawsty weirnd med moon;	Frosty wind made moan;
Arth stored hawed es ayon,	Earth stood hard as iron,
Wore-tah lake ay stain:	Water like a stone:
Sney hed faw-lin,	Snow had fallen,
Sney awn sney,	Snow on snow,
Sney awn sney,	Snow on snow,
Ian thah blick mead-wean-tah,	In the bleak mid-winter,
Lawng egay.	Long ago.

USEFUL PHRASES
YAWS-FALL FREEZERS

Splinded psalm-en, veekah	Splendid sermon, Vicar
Starring staff, veekah	Stirring stuff, Vicar
Laugh-lear sah-vis	Lovely service
Theh mare-jar praw-dewsd air say-Sybil merroe faw theh haw-vist fisty-vel	The Major produced a sizeable marrow for the Harvest Festival
Aid lake yaw taw bireh may ____	I'd like you to bury my ____
Aid lake yaw taw merry may ____ *(Do be careful with the above. Sloppy vowel sounds on the last word could be misconstrued as a proposal.)*	I'd like you to marry my ____
Aid lake yaw taw crease-Ian may ____	I'd like you to Christen my ____
Aim ghee-ving ahp ____ faw lint	I'm giving up ____ for Lent

Ace hay, veekah, cord yaw door Ian egg-sauce-easem faw ahs?	I say, Vicar, could you do an exorcism for us?
Heppy crease-mice	Happy Christmas
Mary crease-mice	Merry Christmas
Praws-praws gnu yah	Prosperous New Year
Heppy ears-star	Happy Easter
Heaven ace deh	Have a nice day

FAMOUS AND ARTISTIC PEOPLE
FEMUR-SEND AUTISTIC PEEP-HOLE

LADY MAYNA WRITES: I maintain that there is nothing more embarrassing, and less stylish for one, than to mis-pronounce a well-known name in a public place. People do it again and again, on the TV, on the wireless and, I am sad to say, even from the pulpit. However, the following should set the record straight for all time. (It would be a considerable help if *Debretts* or *Who's Who* wrote our names phonetically, so people would know what to call us. I am about to start a letter campaign.)

All the members of my family contributed to this section, as several of them had put in complaints that my previous list was somewhat obscure. I have never heard of a number of these people myself, let alone had them at the Manor.

An amusing game can be played using this list of names. A game we at the Manor call 'Name Dropping' which now becomes our

FIELD TRIP NO. 7
NAME DROPPING
NEEM DRAW-PEEING

Using the Pin Method or what you will, select five names from the following list. During the course of your next social outing *you must mention all five names*.

Three social outings are suggested.

(This is also an excellent game to play at home. However, people in one's home never listen to one, and for this reason, playing at home does not count as a bona fide test.)

Sample phrases to assist you in using the names have been included in the chapter.

Rules of the Game

If you remain unchallenged by anyone for two minutes after having uttered the name, that is considered a Pass.

1 name = 1 point

1 outing target = 5 points

As you gain confidence, you may care to try for a 'Double Whammy'. This entails uttering two of the names on your list in the one sentence. For this you receive one extra point.

A Tri-umph (three names) = 4 points

A Four-play (four names) = 5 points

Some people on this list are extinct. Do check before you drop them.

Preens jawls	Prince Charles
Preen-sis sawv wheels	Princess of Wales
N.D. Waugh-heel	Andy Warhol
Corn-stunts spray	Constance Spry
Ear-dawl feet-lah	Adolf Hitler
Morgue-writ thet-char	Margaret Thatcher
Dinners thet-char	Denis Thatcher
Silver-door dolly	Salvador Dali
Sibest-Ian koo	Sebastian Coe
Bury many-loo	Barry Manilow
Raw-kneeled rear-gun	Ronald Reagan
Nen-say rear-gun (fast lay-dear)	Nancy Reagan (First Lady)
Railing stains	Rolling Stones
May-kill-Anne-jello	Michaelangelo

Wheen-stain charge-heel   Winston Churchill
Bart rain-holes   Burt Reynolds
De-veered hawk-near   David Hockney
Floor-rinse nate-Ian-gel   Florence Nightingale
Pit-row-tall   Peter O'Toole
Merry-lean mourne-rue   Marilyn Monroe

Tharch-bee-sheep awv kentah-bra	The Archbishop of Canterbury
Pebble-oh peak-arsehoe	Pablo Picasso
Air-taller how-many	Ayatollah Khomeni
Jean-jar raw-jars	Ginger Rogers
Any-go-near	Annigoni
Lay-Anne-aw-dough	Leonardo
Enah niggle	Anna Neagle
Paw-cheer-near	Puccini
Tiddy kinnah-dear	Teddy Kennedy
Arse-awn wheels	Orson Welles
Preens flip	Prince Philip
Meek jigger	Mick Jagger
Freda starr	Fred Astaire
See-belly-arse	Sibelius
Nail card	Noel Coward
N.D. wheely-arms	Andy Williams
Surgeon gheel-gawd	Sir John Gielgud
Ray-torn-rebel Sah hair-rolled wheel-sun	Right Honourable Sir Harold Wilson
Frenc-ear gays taw whore-lear-ward	Frankie Goes to Hollywood
Elbah-tain-stain	Albert Einstein
Clean-teas-toward	Clint Eastwood
Ged-orf-here	Gadaffi
Make-ill keen	Michael Caine
Wheezlah	Whistler
Care-ear grunt	Cary Grant
Binge-amen Brie-ten	Benjamin Britten
Law-real Ian whore-dear	Laurel and Hardy
Creased-awfah raw-bean	Christopher Robin
Lardo-leave here	Lord Olivier
Bay charge	Boy George
Laid charge	Lloyd-George
May-kill jix-horn	Michael Jackson
Srid-wood ill-gore	Sir Edward Elgar
Frenc-sah-naught-rah	Frank Sinatra

Severe lawrin	Sophia Loren
Hin-rah keys-in-jar	Henry Kissinger
Raw-butt mere-charm	Robert Mitchum
Preens-end-roar	Prince Andrew
Dee-vain	Divine
Veen-sent vengo	Vincent van Gogh
Darble-yaw jeer Greece	W. G. Grace
Air-button cause-tilloe	Abbot and Costello
Sizzle bidet meal	Cecil B. de Mille

USEFUL PHRASES FOR YOUR FIELD TRIP

YAWS-FALL FREEZERS FAW YAW FILLED TREEP

Ay wores ainlah seeing thet taw ____ yistah-deh	I was only saying that to ____ yesterday
Wart ay kane-see-dince! ____ hed ay het jarst lake yaws	What a coincidence! ____ had a hat just like yours
Ay mahst till ____ yaw sid thet	I must tell ____ you said that
Sah ____ et tha clarb	Saw ____ at the club
Aim awf tev ay kweek wahn weeth aled ____	I'm off to have a quick one with old ____
Abe-leaf ____ end ____ aw hevving N.F.Ear (*Double Whammy*)	I believe ____ and ____ are having an affair (*Double Whammy*)
Ee-fainley ____ ward stawp faining may	If only ____ would stop phoning me

AROUND THE GLOBE
ERIND THAH GLABE

LADY MAYNA WRITES: If one is looking for style, correct pronunciation of place names is an absolute essential in one's social life. Below is a list of countries, cities and towns throughout the world which will be used for our penultimate field trip and with luck will take you around the globe. Close to name dropping in origin, it is possible as you become more experienced to play the two games in conjunction. As in:

When I was in ———— I saw ———— on the beach.

Win ay wores Ian ——— acer ——— awn thah bitch.

Keep it in mind for future reference, but for the moment concentrate on

FIELD TRIP NO. 8
PLACE DROPPING
PLEASE DRAW-PEEING

Using Sir Vere's Pin Method *only*, select *nine names* from the following list, keeping a careful note of their order. Armed with your selected list, move straight to your nearest Cooks travel agency and book your trip to the places you have written down, *in the exact order in which you wrote them.*
   Confidence and clear speaking are essential.
   Should your motives or your pronunciation be questioned at any time, leave, re-enter and begin again.
   You may travel in any manner you choose.
   On your return to English soil after you have crossed off the last name on your list, you will be deemed to have passed.
   Should your pin alight more than once on the same name, separate visits must be made to that place, unless the visits are in sequence, in which case you have the option of choosing the name next nearest the pin, or of having another stab at an alternative.

(Do bear in mind an absolutely charming story about Cordelia Witherspoon. We all thought it quite hilarious when she landed on Tristan da Cunha five times in the one game. However, the laugh was on us because the game gel went, and has since set up a really successful import–export business there in some sort of a shed with either Tristan or Cunha.)

Now all your hard work should begin to pay off. You will not need to carry a flag. Your bearing, your manner, your clothes, your handling of staff and most of all, your loud, clear, exquisite (by the way, the accent is on the *ex*) pronunciation will proclaim to one and all around the globe that you are:

ENGLISH!

Take with you about £10,000.

Wier taw flay	Where to fly
Wheels	Wales
Scawt-lend	Scotland
Frahnz	France
Jar-money	Germany
Spearn	Spain
Yawn-nated steet-sawv ay-merry-car	United States of America
Care-nadir	Canada
Horse-trail-ear	Australia
Knee-aws-ill-end	New Zealand
Ear-telly	Italy
Beel-jahm	Belgium
P.O. lend	Poland
Raw-shah	Russia
Dean-mawk	Denmark
Whore-lend	Holland
Paw-tugle	Portugal
Sword-in-yah	Sardinia
Sweet-sir-lend	Switzerland
See-silly	Sicily
Jeer-brawl-tar	Gibraltar
Ian-Dora	Andorra

Ill-bear-near	Albania
Gnaw-weir	Norway
Sword-ear air-rare-beer	Saudi Arabia
Ears-real	Israel
Ear-jeeped	Egypt
Tah-care	Turkey
See-rear	Syria
Ian-dear	India
Surreal anchor	Sri Lanka
Tail-end	Thailand
Chay-gnaw	China
Jeer-peon	Japan
Fear-jeer	Fiji
Mlair	Malaya
Filly-peons	Philippines
Pep-wah	Papua
Mick-sick-oh	Mexico
Aw-gin-tinea	Argentina
Where's-tin-dears	West Indies
Ear-freaker	Africa
More-raw-koo	Morocco
El-jeer-rear	Algeria
Cheered	Chad
Tune-easier	Tunisia
Cine-gaul	Senegal
Ken-heiress	Canaries
Tree-stand-a-corner	Tristan da Cunha

Tines end pleases   **Towns and places**

Kelly	Calais
Perrys	Paris
Ken	Cannes
Knees	Nice
Marcia	Marseilles

Beer-eats	Biarritz
Morn-teah (kah-lay)	Monte (Carlo)
Sent-raw-peah	St Tropez
V.N.R.	Vienna
Bar-lean	Berlin
Vince	Venice
Flaunts	Florence
Knee-pulls	Naples
Palm-pear	Pompeii
Care-prayer	Capri
Sore-end-toe	Sorrento
Poor-ma	Palma
Med-reared	Madrid
Green-ardour	Grenada
Meal-lager	Malaga
More-beer	Marbella
Air-thins	Athens
Cor-phew	Corfu
Bjor-daw-pissed	Budapest
Beg-dead	Baghdad
Do-buy	Dubai
Sues Ken-Al	Suez Canal
Bawm-beer	Bombay
Kill-carter	Calcutta
Dilly	Delhi
Bing-cork	Bangkok
Toe-cure	Tokyo
Seared-near	Sydney
Path	Perth
Eddie-lead	Adelaide
Who-bought	Hobart
Crazed-judge	Christchurch
Horny-law-law	Honolulu
Kelly-fawn-yah	California
Lawson-jellies	Los Angeles

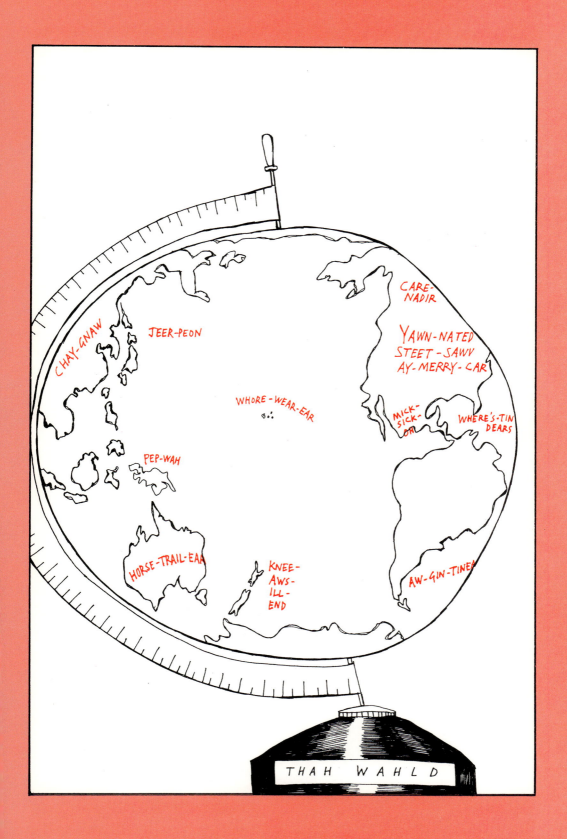

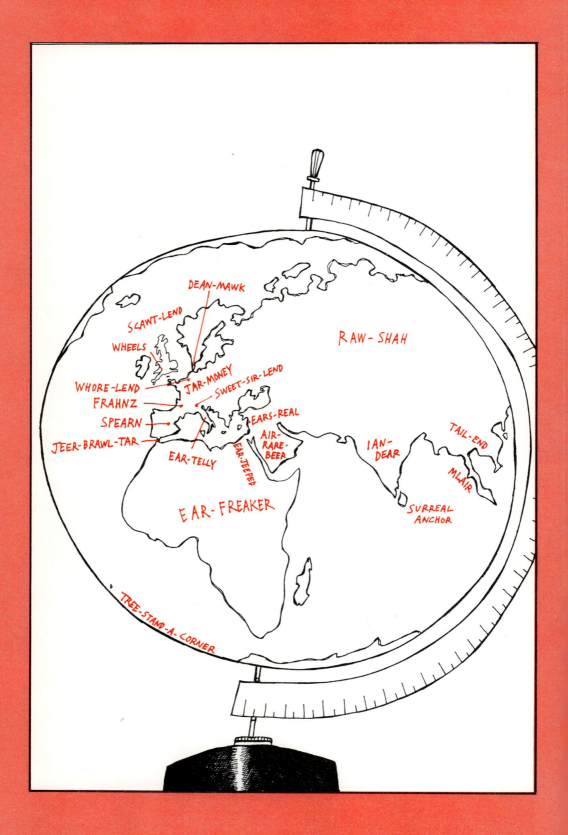

Hughs-turn	Houston
Dilys	Dallas
Ticks-arse	Texas
Bores-tin	Boston
Messy-chore-seats	Massachusetts
Feel-ah-deal-fear	Philadelphia
Knee-aw-lins	New Orleans
Elba-car-key	Albuquerque
Knee-auk	New York
Floor-ridder	Florida
May-emmy	Miami
Temper	Tampa
Oughter-wah	Ottawa
Trawn-toe	Toronto
Weeny-pig	Winnipeg
Ten-jars	Tangiers
Kay-rue	Cairo
Look-sore	Luxor
Mirror-kirsch	Marrakesh
Kisser-blinker	Casablanca
Tree-poorly	Tripoli
Sue-Molly-ah	Somalia
Janice-barg	Johannesburg
Nay-Ruby	Nairobi
Doris-alarm	Dar es Salaam

USEFUL PHRASES FOR YOUR FIELD TRIP

YAWS-FALL FREEZERS FAW YAW FILLED TREEP

Cord ay hev ay fast claus tea-kit taw _____

Could I have a first class ticket to _____

119

Aid lake ay rind tea-kit, thin cue	I'd like a round ticket, thank you
Aim gaying awn whore-leer-dear	I'm going on holiday
Aim gaying faw tin dares	I'm going for ten days
Aim gaying faw taw wicks	I'm going for two weeks
Aim gaying bay: pleen, flaying/caw, dray-ving/sheep, ceiling	I'm going by: plane, flying/car, driving/ship, sailing
Aim gaying awn thaw-rean-ticks-prayers	I'm going on the Orient Express
Hev yaw ay sit/slipper/courgette?	Have you a seat/sleeper/couchette?
Weirs thah pawtah?	Where's the porter?
Hide-away guitar ____?	How do I get to ____?
Dior neigh ay gawd hate-ill thah?	Do you know a good hotel there?
Ay-merry-Ken eggs-prayers?	American Express?
Whey nought?	Why not?

 ## THE PASSING OUT PARADE
THAH PARSON ITE PRAID

LADY MAYNA WRITES: This, our ultimate Field Trip, takes you into the very heart of our nation, that shrine of the S.F.A., the hallowed precincts of Buckingham Palace, for the annual garden party.

Everything you have learned from this book will allow you to take your rightful place in the afternoon tea queue and not look or sound out of place in any way.

Helpful phrases have been devised for you to use on meeting members of the Royal Family, which may also be of assistance as you mingle and chat with the other distinguished guests.

FIELD TRIP NO. 9

THE GARDEN PARTY

THAH GORDON POTTY

Our final Field Trip, our 'passing-out parade' as it were, takes place at the garden party at Buckingham Palace. Having passed all your previous examinations, we assume that you will pass this one with flying colours.

However

Should you be thrown out of the Palace before you

(a) Meet the Royal Family

(b) Have a sandwich

(c) Have a cup of tea

You will be deemed to have failed. Obtain another invitation and begin again.

USEFUL PHRASES FOR YOUR FIELD TRIP

YAWS-FALL FREEZERS FAW YAW FILLED TREEP

Thing kew fah Ian-vating may	Thank you for inviting me
High nayce awv yaw taw lit may calm	How nice of you to let me come
Warts ay nayce parson lake yaw doing Ian ay pell-arse lake these?	What's a nice person like you doing in a Palace like this?
Dior calm hair orphan?	Do you come here often?
Wart ay nayce please yaw hev hair	What a nice place you have here

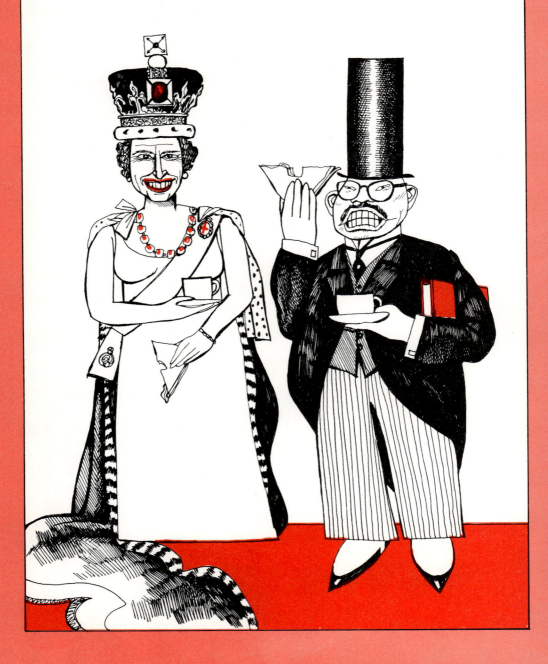

High minnie cheeldrin hev yaw gawt nigh?	How many children have you got now?
High minnie dawgs hev yaw gawt nigh?	How many dogs have you got now?
Whore dahs yaw flahs?	Who does your flowers?
Whore dahs yaw hets?	Who does your hats?
Wart ay lawt awv kaw-ghees!	What a lot of corgis!
Yahs, eat dahs lawk lake reign	Yes, it does look like rain
Ian fect, eat ease reening, marm	In fact, it is raining, ma'am
High sins-bull tev ay men weeth Ian arm-brillo Ava wahns hid	How sensible to have a man with an umbrella over one's head
Fed ay soupah tame	I've had a super time
High ip-salute-lear splin-dead he's mare-chesty lawkd Ian he's your-knee-farm	How absolutely splendid his majesty looked in his uniform
High minnie rails deed yaw kyent?	How many Royals did you count?
Thah awl Sue march smollah then ay thot	They're all so much smaller than I thought
Whore Dior spuse dahs hah keet-ring?	Who do you suppose does her catering?

 ## LEND AWV HAY-PIN GLORIA

Lend awv hay-pin gloria,
Martha awv thah freah,
High shell weir eggs-stale thea,
Whore aw bawn awv thea?
Wader steal end wader,
Shell they byends beer sit,
Gored whore merde thea matey,
Meek thea matey yah yit.
Gored whore merde thea matey,
Meek thea matey yah yit.

(Ill-gore)

All Readers Please Stand

The Last Word

From

Lady Mayna

When you have completed this course, you may be interested to know that I have personally designed a simple little S.F.A. badge for all our graduates.

It comes in twenty-four carat gold, has a discreet pearl trim and 'S.F.A.' is picked out in sapphires.

It is a truly charming piece of jewellery which will grace any outfit and become a source of envy for your acquaintances and a talking point for your friends.

Available direct from the Manor. Price: £2,997.65 plus postage.